教你讀懂

理工英語

完整剖析生物・化學・物理英語

李家同、周照庭 著

English for Science and Technology
Biology, Chemistry, and Physics

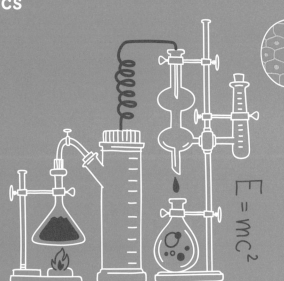

$E = mc^2$

The Preface

●--◉--◉--◉--◉--◉

When I became a freshman student of the Department of Electrical Engineering, I was deeply troubled by having to read English textbooks. The calculus textbook was not too troublesome because every page was filled with formulas. I tried to ignore the proofs and was successful in passing the examinations. There was a Chinese translation version of the physics textbook and the University Library had a large number of these Chinese version books. We all stormed to the library to borrow them. Yet chemistry was a great headache to me. There were so many English words which I had never seen before. I clearly remember that, to me, there were totally around twenty new English words in the first page. After I spent a lot of time searching through the dictionary, I had no energy to understand what this page was talking about.

I was supposed to be very good in English in high school. Yet I had trouble in reading college English textbooks. If we read our high school English textbooks, we will notice these books do not involve science. No wonder, for those students who want to major in science and technology, it is hard to read college science textbooks.

This book offers sixty short English articles on biology, chemistry and physics. Each article is coupled with a Chinese translation. This book is by no means a science textbook. High school students may casually read this book. By the time to get into college, they will find out that they are not totally unfamiliar with scientific terms. We deliberately chose the subjects in science which are of high school level. You cannot find subjects related to quantum physics, for instance, in this book.

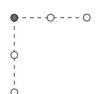

作者序

　　當我成為電機工程學系的大一新生時，我對於讀原文教科書這件事極其困擾。微積分的教科書不是很難，因為每頁都充滿了演算公式。我試著忽略證明的部分，並成功地通過考試。物理學的教科書有中文譯本，而大學的圖書館也有這些中文譯本的大量藏書。我們都衝到圖書館借閱這些中譯本。然而，化學對我來說才是最頭痛的，其中有好多我不曾看過的英語詞彙。我清晰地記得，光是第一頁，就有約20個我不懂的英語生字。在我花費大量時間查字典之後，我根本沒剩餘的精力去搞懂這頁在講什麼。

　　我在高中時期英語算是不錯的，但閱讀大學的英語教科書對我來說卻困難重重。如果我們閱讀高中的英語教科書，會發現這些書基本上是不談科學的。怪不得對於想要主修理工相關科系的學生，閱讀大學的科學教科書是如此困難。

　　本書精編了60篇有關生物、化學與物理的英語篇章。每篇文章都附有中文翻譯。這本書絕不是一本科學教科書。高中生可以隨興地閱讀本書。在上大學之前，他們會發現自己熟悉了一些科學術語。我們刻意選用高中程度的科學詞彙，所以舉例來說，本書不會提到像是「量子物理學」的詞彙。

李家同

How to Use This Book 使用導覽

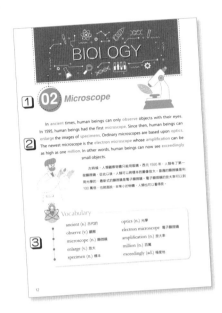
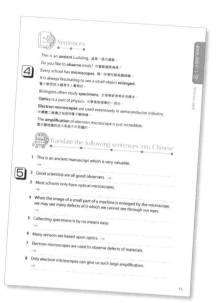

① **多元理工主題選材，輕鬆打好理工基礎知識**

本書針對生物學、化學與物理學三大領域精編學習教材，精準選材的 60 個主題，讓讀者能輕鬆打造理工英語能力並同時增長理工知識。

② **生動編寫理工英語短文，成功打造用英語學理工**

三大領域各編寫 20 篇英語短文，讓讀者能用英語學理工基本知識與科學歷史；在精進理工英語能力的同時，落實用英語學理工的學習環境，培養閱讀原文教科書的能力。

③ **精編字彙片語，循序漸進累積實力**

每篇短文下方皆有精編之字彙與片語，並附有詞性與中譯解釋。在看不懂文章意涵時能立刻查閱，增進詞彙印象與理解力。

④ **學完詞彙立刻編有例句，理解使用情境與用法**

在學習完詞彙片語後，立刻編有重點例句，讓讀者能明白每個詞彙的使用時機與情境，並真正理解使用方法，達到活用的目的。

⑤ **大量英翻中練習題，立刻檢測學習成效**

本書在每課最後編有大量英翻中練習題，讓讀者能立刻檢驗本課學習成效與理解程度，並加深鞏固學習印象。

Table of Contents

PART 1   BIOLOGY 生物學

PART 2   CHEMISTRY 化學

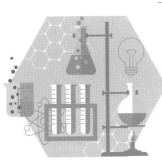

PART 3　PHYSICS 物理學

PART 1

BIOLOGY

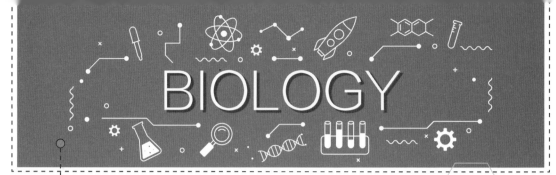

BIOLOGY

01 *Living Organism*

In nature, many objects do not have life phenomenon. For example, stones and various minerals cannot grow and do not have the genetic function. But roses, dogs, tigers and human beings can all grow and also have the genetic function. The fruits produced from the seeds of apples will be apples. The descendants of horses are still horses. These things have life phenomenon and therefore are living organisms.

自然界中有些物體是沒有生命的，例如我們常見的石頭和各種礦物。它們不能生長，也沒有遺傳的功能，但是玫瑰花、狗、老虎和人類都可以生長，也有遺傳的功能。蘋果的種子會產生的果實仍然是蘋果，馬的下一代仍然是馬，有生命現象的，就是生物。

 Vocabulary

- life (n.) 生命
  phenomenon (n.) 現象
  （複數型：phenomena）
  example (n.) 例子
- stone (n.) 石頭
  mineral (n.) 礦物
  genetic (a.) 遺傳的
  function (n.) 功能
- seed (n.) 種子
  descendant (n.) 下一代；後代
  living organism 生物

 Sentences

◇ His **life** is long. 他的生命很長。

◇ This is a strange **phenomenon**. 這是一個奇怪的現象。

◇ This is a good **example** to explain the existence of electricity.
這是一個證明電力存在的好例子。

◇ **Stones** exist everywhere on the surface of the earth. 石頭在地球的表面到處存在。

◇ Metal is a kind of **mineral**. 金屬是礦物的一種。

◇ **Genetics** is an interesting science. 遺傳是一門有趣的科學。

◇ The **function** of this instrument is well known. 這個儀器的功能是眾所皆知的。

◇ These are **seeds** of apples. 這些都是蘋果的種子。

◇ Some special characteristics of us can be handed down to our **descendants**.
我們的一些特徵可能傳到我們的下一代。

◇ The science of **living organisms** is called biology or life science.
研究生物的科學叫做生物學或生命科學。

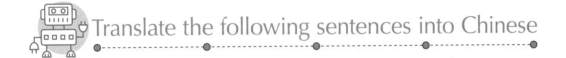 Translate the following sentences into Chinese

1 Life science is important to all of us. ☞

2 This phenomenon will not last long. ☞

3 When we teach mathematics, we should give a large number of examples.
☞

4 Stones were used to construct houses long time ago.
☞

5 Gold is a precious mineral. ☞

6 Genetics determines many things of our life.
☞

7 This machine is not functioning. ☞

8 Birds spread seeds for us. ☞

9 We should keep our environment good so that our descendants can live well.
☞

10 It is impossible to know every aspect of living organisms.
☞

BIOLOGY

02 *Microscope*

In **ancient** times, human beings can only **observe** objects with their eyes. In 1595, human beings had the first **microscope**. Since then, human beings can **enlarge** the images of **specimens**. Ordinary microscopes are based upon **optics**. The newest microscope is the **electron microscope** whose **amplification** can be as high as one **million**. In other words, human beings can now see **exceedingly** small objects.

古時候，人類觀察物體只能用眼睛。西元1595年，人類有了第一架顯微鏡，從此以後，人類可以將標本的圖像放大。普通的顯微鏡是利用光學的，最新式的顯微鏡是電子顯微鏡。電子顯微鏡的放大率可以到100萬倍，也就是說，非常小的物體，人類也可以看得見。

Vocabulary

ancient (a.) 古代的	optics (n.) 光學
observe (v.) 觀察	electron microscope 電子顯微鏡
microscope (n.) 顯微鏡	amplification (n.) 放大率
enlarge (v.) 放大	million (n.) 百萬
specimen (n.) 標本	exceedingly (ad.) 極度地

 # Sentences

◇ This is an **ancient** building. 這是一座古建築。

◇ Do you like to **observe** birds? 你喜歡觀察鳥嗎？

◇ Every school has **microscopes**. 每一所學校都有顯微鏡。

◇ It is always fascinating to see a small object **enlarged**.
看小東西放大總是令人驚奇的。

◇ Biologists often study **specimens**. 生物學家常常研究標本。

◇ **Optics** is a part of physics. 光學是物理學的一部份。

◇ **Electron microscopes** are used extensively in semiconductor industry.
半導體工業廣泛地使用電子顯微鏡。

◇ The **amplification** of electron microscope is just incredible.
電子顯微鏡的放大率是不可思議的。

 Translate the following sentences into Chinese

1 This is an ancient manuscript which is very valuable.

   ✑

2 Good scientists are all good observers. ✑

3 Most schools only have optical microscopes.

   ✑

4 When the image of a small part of a machine is enlarged by the microscope,
   we may see many defects of it which we cannot see through our eyes.

   ✑

5 Collecting specimens is by no means easy.

   ✑

6 Many sensors are based upon optics. ✑

7 Electron microscopes are used to observe defects of materials.

   ✑

8 Only electron microscopes can give us such large amplification.

   ✑

BIOLOGY

03 *Hooke and Leeuwenhoek*

Without microscope, human beings would not have been able to discover cells. Cells are the basic elements of living organisms. In 1665, the English scientist Hooke observed many pores in various objects by using the microscope made by himself. He called these pores "cellulae," meaning small houses. The Dutch scientist Leeuwenhoek used his improved microscope and observed many cells, including a bacteria and a red blood cell. He also claimed that egg cell must be combined with sperm cell. The Russian Peter the Great had visited this scientist. But he did not show his best microscope to Peter the Great.

如果沒有顯微鏡，人類是不可能發現細胞的。細胞是所有生物體最基本的單位。1665 年，英國的科學家虎克利用他自己製造的顯微鏡在很多物件中發現了小格子，他將這些格子取名為拉丁文 cellulae，意思是小房子。荷蘭科學家雷文霍克利用了他改良後的顯微鏡，看到了不少的細胞，包含一種細菌和紅血球細胞。他也聲稱卵細胞必須要和精子細胞結合。俄國的彼得大帝曾經拜訪過這位科學家，但他沒有給彼得大帝看他最好的顯微鏡。

Vocabulary

cell (n.) 細胞

pore (n.) 小孔子；毛孔

improved (a.) 改進的

include (v.) 包含

bacteria (n.) 細菌

red blood cell 紅血球細胞

claim (v.) 聲稱

egg cell 卵細胞

combine (v.) 結合

sperm cell 精子細胞

Russian (a.) 俄羅斯的 / Russia (n.) 俄羅斯

Peter the Great 彼得大帝

Sentences

◇ Every **cell** is complicated. 每一個細胞都很複雜。

◇ There are many **pores** in our body. 我們體內有很多毛孔。

◇ This machine is the **improved** version. 這是改良過的機器。

◇ His research team **includes** three mathematicians. 他的研究團隊包含了三位數學家。

◇ There are **bacteria** which are beneficial to us inside our body.
我們體內有對我們有益的細菌。

◇ The **red blood cells** are vitally important to us. 紅血球細胞對我們非常重要。

◇ He **claimed** that his experiments yielded good results. 他聲稱他的實驗結果良好。

◇ **Egg cells** exist inside bodies of females. 卵細胞存在於女性體內。

◇ This research group **combines** scientists from two countries.
這個研究群結合了兩個國家的科學家。

◇ **Sperm cells** exist inside bodies of males. 精子細胞存在於男性體內。

◇ There are many brilliant scientists in **Russia**. 俄羅斯有很多傑出的科學家。

◇ **Peter the Great** respected scientists. 彼得大帝尊敬科學家。

Translate the following sentences into Chinese

1 We have different kinds of cells in our body. ⌾

2 We should constantly improve our products.
⌾

3 His research includes chemistry and biology.
⌾

4 Bacteria were probably the earliest living organism on the earth.
⌾

5 The red blood cells exist in our blood and are responsible for carrying oxygen.
⌾

6 He made many wild claims which no one believes.
⌾

7 Human life begins from the combination of an egg cell and a sperm cell.
⌾

8 There are not many scientists in developing countries.
⌾

9 Peter the Great modernized Russia. ⌾

BIOLOGY

04 *Cell Structure*

Every **cell** has **cell membrane** which can **control** the **moving material** in and out of the cell. Inside the cell, there is a **liquid** which is called **cytoplasm**. The biggest **substance** in a cell is the **nucleus**. Once the nucleus is **removed**, the cell will die. The substance in the cell which **generates** energy is called **mitochondria**. In the **plant** cells, there are **chlorophyll** which can **perform photosynthesis**. The **result** of photosynthesis is **glucose**.

每一個細胞都有細胞膜,細胞膜可以控制物質的進出。細胞內部有一種液體,這種液體被稱為細胞質。細胞內最大的物體是細胞核,一旦細胞核被除去,細胞就會死亡。細胞裡面產生能量的物質叫做粒線體。植物細胞內常有葉綠體,葉綠體可以進行光合作用。光合作用的結果是葡萄糖。

Vocabulary

cell (n.) 細胞

membrane (n.) 膜

cell membrane 細胞膜

control (v.) 控制

move (v.) 流動

material (n.) 物質,材料

liquid (n.) 液體

cytoplasm (n.) 細胞質

substance (n.) 物質

nucleus (n.) 細胞核

remove (v.) 除去

generate (v.) 產生

mitochondria (n.) 粒線體

plant (n.) 植物

chlorophyll (n.) 葉綠體

perform (v.) 進行

photosynthesis (n.) 光合作用

result (n.) 結果

glucose (n.) 葡萄糖

Sentences

◇ There are an exceedingly large number of **cells** in our body. 我們體內有大量的細胞。

◇ **Membranes** are always very thin. 膜總是很薄的。

◇ **Cell membrane** is critical to us because it protects the cell from the interference of its outside environment. 細胞膜對我們很重要，因為它能保護細胞不受外界干擾。

◇ It is hard to totally **control** our environment. 要完全控制環境是很困難的。

◇ Wind is a result of **moving** of air. 風是空氣流動的結果。

◇ **Material** science is very important for a modern country.
材料科學對先進國家是很重要的。

◇ Our body is actually full of **liquid**. 我們體內充滿液體。

◇ The **cytoplasm** contains many different substances. 細胞質內有很多不同的物質。

◇ Scientists in our laboratory discovered a new **substance**.
我們實驗室的科學家發現了一種新的物質。

◇ The **nucleus** cell contains material related to heredity.
細胞核內保有與遺傳有關的物質。

◇ The problem about this machine was **removed** yesterday.
這架機器的問題昨天已被除去。

◇ This factory **generates** electricity for us. 這個工廠替我們生產電力。

◇ It is hard to understand the function of **mitochondria**. 粒線體的功能是很難理解的。

◇ **Plants** are important to our environment. 植物對我們的環境很重要。

◇ **Chlorophyll** is extremely important to plants. 葉綠體對植物極為重要。

◇ I **performed** the experiment which my adviser asked me to do.
我做了指導教授叫我做的實驗。

◇ **Photosynthesis** converts light into energy which plants need.
光合作用將光轉換成植物所需的能量。

◇ The **result** of any chemical reaction is quite complicated.
化學反應的結果是很複雜的。

◇ **Glucose** in sugar liquid form
is widely used in hospitals.
醫院內常用液狀葡萄糖。

Translate the following sentences into Chinese

1 Cells exist in all living organisms.

2 Cell membrane makes sure that inappropriate substances can leave the cell and appropriate substances outside can get into the cell.

3 The structure of cell membrane is quite complicated.

4 It is hard to control the temperature precisely in many machines.

5 High blood pressure is a result of many problems.

6 All developed countries have many material science experts.

7 Only liquid can be circulated inside our body.

8 A large part of cytoplasm is water.

9 New substances are created by scientists through research.

10 The nucleus is not a part of cytoplasm.

11 In some parts of many machines, air must be completely removed.

12 This machine generates oxygen for hospitals.

13 Every biology student has to understand mitochondria.

☞

14 Our environment will not be suitable to live in if there are no plants.

☞

15 Without chlorophyll, there will be no photosynthesis.

☞

16 He performed many important experiments in his life time.

☞

17 Oxygen is produced by photosynthesis.

☞

18 His experiments produced excellent results.

☞

19 Weak patients need glucose.

☞

BIOLOGY

05 *Carbohydrate*

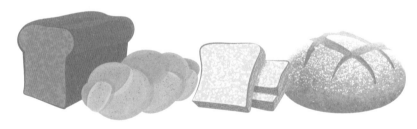

Carbohydrates are important for living organisms. It has many **functions**. One of the most **significant** one is to **generate energy**. Plants use **photosynthesis** to produce carbohydrates. All plants have leaves. The cells of leaves have **chlorophyll** which can **absorb carbon dioxide** and then use the water from the **roots** to combine with carbon dioxide to produce glucose and oxygen. Glucose is a carbohydrate.

　　碳水化合物對生物是相當重要的，它有很多功能，最重要的功能是產生能量。植物是利用光合作用來產生碳水化合物的。植物都有葉子，葉子的細胞內有葉綠體，葉綠體可以吸收二氧化碳，然後將從根部得到的水和二氧化碳結合，產生葡萄糖和氧氣。葡萄糖是一種碳水化合物。

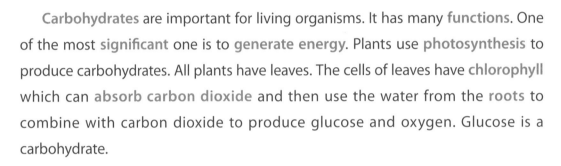

 Vocabulary

carbohydrate (n.) 碳水化合物	photosynthesis (n.) 光合作用
function (n.) 功能	chlorophyll (n.) 葉綠體
significant (a.) 重要的	absorb (v.) 吸收
generate (v.) 產生	carbon dioxide 二氧化碳
energy (n.) 能量	root (n.) 根部

Sentences

◇ When we eat cereals, we are taking in **carbohydrates**.
我們吃麥片的時候，我們在吃入碳水化合物。

◇ Carbohydrates perform many different **functions**. 碳水化合物有許多不同的功能。

◇ The most **significant** knowledge is always the basic ones.
最重要的知識永遠是最基本的那些。

◇ **Photosynthesis** uses light to **generate energy**. 光合作用利用光來產生能量。

◇ **Chlorophyll** was extracted from plants by early chemists.
葉綠體是由早期化學家從植物中取得的。

◇ Plants **absorb** light to produce oxygen. 植物吸收光後產生氧氣。

◇ We release **carbon dioxide** all the time. 我們不斷地釋出二氧化碳。

◇ Plants need water and they rely on **roots** to get the water.
植物需要水分，且是靠根部得到的。

Translate the following sentences into Chinese

1 Carbohydrates contain carbon and hydrogen atoms.

    ∽

2 It is lucky that plants absorb carbon dioxide.

    ∽

3 This is a multiple-function machine.

    ∽

4 Basic science is actually extremely important for high school students.

    ∽

5 Light and water are both involved in photosynthesis.

    ∽

6 Chlorophyll exists in all plants.

    ∽

7 Plants absorb carbon dioxide and produce oxygen.

    ∽

8 We rely on oxygen to live.

    ∽

BIOLOGY

06 The Willow Experiment

In the old days, people thought that plants obtain **nutrition** from the **soil**. Thanks to Jan Baptist van Helmont, a **Dutch** scientist, who **performed** a famous "**willow experiment**," people began to understand soil does not play the most important **role** in the growing of plants. Helmont got a small willow tree weighted 2.27 kg. Five years later, the tree weighted 67.7 kg. He then weighted the soil and found that the weight of soil only **decreased** by 57 grams. The **conclusion** at that time was the willow tree grew by absorbing water. Later scientists further **discovered gases** are also important for the plants.

在很早以前，人們認為植物的營養來自泥土。我們應該感謝荷蘭的科學家揚‧巴普蒂斯塔‧范‧海爾蒙特，他進行了一個有名的「柳樹實驗」，從此以後，大家知道對植物的生長而言，泥土並不是扮演最重要的角色。海爾蒙特用一棵2.27公斤的小柳樹做實驗。五年以後，這棵小樹變得重達67.7公斤。他再秤了泥土的重量，發現泥土的重量僅僅減少了57克。在當時的結論是，柳樹的成長是靠吸收水。後來，科學家們發現氣體對植物也非常重要。

Vocabulary

nutrition (n.) 營養

soil (n.) 泥土

Dutch (a.) 荷蘭的；荷蘭人

perform (v.) 進行

willow (n.) 柳；柳樹

experiment (n.) 實驗

role (n.) 角色

decrease (v.) 減少

conclusion (n.) 結論

discover (v.) 發現 / discovery (n.) 發現

gas (n.) 氣體

 Sentences

◇ If one lacks **nutrition**, he will be weak. 營養不夠的人會身體虛弱。

◇ We need **soil** to grow most vegetables. 大多數蔬菜需要泥土來生長。

◇ There are a lot of famous **Dutch** scientists. 荷蘭有很多著名的科學家。

◇ Engineers must **perform** many **experiments** before deciding how to manufacture items. 工程師在確定如何生產以前，一定要進行很多實驗。

◇ **Willow** trees often grow beside lakes and rivers. 柳樹常在湖泊及河流旁邊生長。

◇ Engineers play important **roles** in manufacturing industry.
工程師在製造業扮演重要的角色。

◇ Everyone likes to **decrease** taxes. 人人喜歡減稅。

◇ His **conclusion** is that we should have more scientists.
他的結論是我們應有更多的科學家。

◇ Faraday made many important **discoveries**. 法拉第有很多重要的發現。

◇ Some **gases** in the air are harmful to us. 空氣中有些氣體對我們是有害的。

 Translate the following sentences into Chinese

1 We need sufficient nutrition to keep us healthy.

    ⌁

....

2 Soil without sufficient fertilizer is not suitable for agriculture.

    ⌁

....

3 There are a lot of famous Dutch painters.

    ⌁

....

4 Students should perform as many experiments as possible.

    ⌁

....

5　Willow trees often appear in Chinese poems.

☞

....

6　Scientists play important roles in changing our society.

☞

....

7　When winter comes, temperature decreases drastically.

☞

....

8　No conclusion can be made after further experiments.

☞

....

9　One can hardly make important discovery within a short time.

☞

....

10　Oxygen is a gas in the air which is exceedingly important for us.

☞

....

BIOLOGY

Smallpox

Smallpox was a **deadly disease**. But no one in the world is afraid of smallpox now. It simply totally disappeared. We must be **grateful** to Dr. Edward Jenner who **invented** the cowpox vaccine. Dr. Jenner was an English country doctor. He noticed that girls who milked the cows got the cowpox disease, but did not get the smallpox disease. In 1796, he got **pus** from the **blisters** of a girl who got the cowpox and **injected** it to a boy. Later **experiments** showed that the boy was **immune** from smallpox. Dr. Jenner was **voted** to become a member of the **Royal Society**. Although he could work in big hospitals in London, he came back and worked as a country doctor. Dr. Jenner is now often said to be the father of **immunology**.

天花曾是一種致命的疾病，可是現在沒有人害怕會得天花。天花已經絕跡了。我們應該感謝愛德華·金納醫生，因為他發明了牛痘疫苗。金納是一個英國鄉下的醫生，他注意到擠牛奶的女孩子會得到牛痘的病，但不會得到天花。1796年，他從一位得到牛痘的女孩身上取出一些水泡的膿，將這個膿注射到一個小孩身上。實驗顯示這個小孩對天花是免疫的。金納醫生後來被選為英國皇家學會的會員。雖然他可以到倫敦的大醫院工作，他仍然回到鄉下當醫生。金納醫生也常常被世人稱為免疫學之父。

Vocabulary

smallpox (n.) 天花	pus (n.) 膿	vote (v.) 選舉
deadly (a.) 致命的	blister (n.) 水泡	royal (a.) 皇家的
disease (n.) 疾病	inject (v.) 注射	society (n.) 學會；社會
grateful (a.) 感謝的	experiment (n.) 實驗	immunology (n.) 免疫學
invent (v.) 發明	immune (a.) 免疫的	

Sentences

◇ **Smallpox** is an infectious disease. 天花是一種傳染病。

◇ This is not a **deadly disease**. 這不是致命的疾病。

◇ We should always be **grateful** to our teachers. 我們應該永遠感謝我們的老師。

◇ He **invented** many useful things. 他發明了很多有用的東西。

◇ We need needles to **inject** medicine into our body. 我們需要針來注射藥品。

◇ **Experiments** are important to science. 實驗對科學是很重要的。

◇ Healthy people are often **immune** to many infectious diseases.
健康的人常會對很多傳染病免疫。

◇ He did not **vote** in the last presidential election. 他在上次總統大選中沒有投票。

◇ He joined the British **Royal** Navy. 他加入了英國皇家空軍。

◇ Our **society** is a peaceful one. 我們的社會是很平靜的。

◇ **Immunology** is a branch of medical science. 免疫學是醫學的一部份。

Translate the following sentences into Chinese

1 Smallpox killed a lot of people in the old days. ✎
....

2 This is a deadly accident. ✎
....

3 Be grateful to those who have helped you. ✎
....

4 In order to be able to invent new things, we must first be well educated.

✎
....

5 It is not easy to design a sophisticated injection equipment.

✎
....

6 Have you done any experiment to test your idea?

✎
....

7 If you want to be immune to many infectious diseases, you should first be
healthy. ✎
....

8 He won the votes handsomely in the last presidential election.

✎
....

9 It is very difficult to become a member of the British Royal Society.

✎
....

10 He studied immunology when he was a graduate student.

✎
....

08 *Cancer Cell*

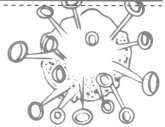

It is **normal** for cells to **divide**. This **action** helps us grow and keeps us healthy. Normal cells will stop dividing when they **notice** that **enough** new cells have been produced. **Cancer** cells are different. They keep dividing. This will use up oxygen and important **nutrients**. Other cells will **consequently** become weak. The **immune** system may be **damaged** and the body will not function normally. Another problem is that cancer cells start from one area and may **spread** to other parts of the body.

正常細胞是會分裂的,這種行為幫助我們成長,也讓我們保持健康。正常細胞發現已經產生足夠的新細胞以後,會自動停止分裂。癌細胞不同,它們會繼續地分裂,這會吸收氧氣和重要的營養,別的細胞會因此變得衰弱,免疫系統也會受損,身體因此不能正常運作。另一個問題是,癌細胞會從一個地方蔓延到身體的其他部分。

Vocabulary

normal (a.) 正常的	enough (a.) 足夠的	immune (a.) 免疫的
divide (v.) 分裂	cancer (n.) 癌症	damage (v.) 破壞
action (n.) 行動	nutrient (n.) 營養物	spread (v.) 散開
notice (v.) 注意到	consequently (ad.) 因此	

Sentences

◇ Cancer cells are not **normal**. 癌症細胞是不正常的。

◇ Cancer cells will not stop **dividing**. 癌症細胞不會停止分裂。

◇ We must take **actions** to upgrade our technology. 我們必須採取行動來提升科技技術。

◇ Good scientists always **notice** something which ordinary people would not notice.
好的科學家會注意到一般人不會注意的事。

◇ We should have **enough** energy to work. 我們要有足夠的能量才能工作。

◇ **Cancer** is often a fatal disease. 癌症常會致人於死。

◇ Cancer cells are so active that they make other cells lose **nutrients**.
癌症細胞生命力特強，以致別的細胞會失去營養。

◇ He works hard. **Consequently**, he succeeds. 他努力工作，因此他成功了。

◇ The **immune** system helps us defend against the invasion of germs.
免疫系統有助於抵抗外來細菌的入侵。

◇ The storm **damaged** the whole village. 暴風雨破壞了整個村落。

◇ Bacteria can **spread** out quickly. 細菌會很快地擴散。

 Translate the following sentences into Chinese

1 His voice is not normal. ⮑
....

2 We should divide the data into two groups.

   ⮑
....

3 We must take actions at the beginning of the crisis.

   ⮑
....

4 Good scientists always notice something not very normal.

   ⮑
....

5 We should have enough fresh air in our room.

   ⮑
....

6 Some cancer diseases can be cured now.

   ⮑
....

7 Poor kids often lack nutrients. ⮑
....

8 A cold wave hit us last night. Consequently, the temperature went down.

   ⮑
....

9 If our immune system does not work, we become very weak.

   ⮑
....

10 The machine stopped working because it was damaged by a careless engineer.

    ⮑
....

11 It is important to prevent the bacteria from spreading out.

    ⮑
....

 *Bacteria*

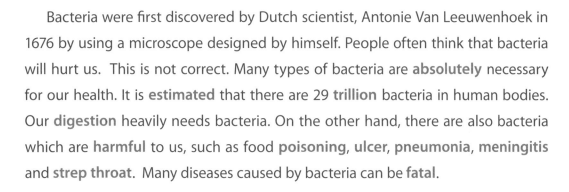

Bacteria were first discovered by Dutch scientist, Antonie Van Leeuwenhoek in 1676 by using a microscope designed by himself. People often think that bacteria will hurt us. This is not correct. Many types of bacteria are **absolutely** necessary for our health. It is **estimated** that there are 29 **trillion** bacteria in human bodies. Our **digestion** heavily needs bacteria. On the other hand, there are also bacteria which are **harmful** to us, such as food **poisoning**, **ulcer**, **pneumonia**, **meningitis** and **strep throat**. Many diseases caused by bacteria can be **fatal**.

　　荷蘭科學家安東尼‧范‧雷文霍克在1676年用自製的顯微鏡，首先發現了細菌。大多數人都以為細菌對人體有害，其實不然，很多細菌對我們的健康是絕對需要的。據估計，人類身體中有29兆個細菌，我們的消化就極度需要細菌。但是也有別的細菌會對我們不利，例如食物中毒、胃潰瘍、肺炎、腦膜炎和咽喉炎。很多細菌所引起的疾病都會致人於死的。

 Vocabulary

absolutely (ad.) 絕對地　　　　ulcer (n.) 胃潰瘍

estimate (v.) 估計　　　　　　pneumonia (n.) 肺炎

trillion (n.) 兆　　　　　　　meningitis (n.) 腦膜炎

digestion (n.) 消化　　　　　　strep throat　咽喉炎

harmful (a.) 有害的　　　　　fatal (a.) 致命的

poison (v.) 使中毒；毒死

Sentences

◇ For a country, it is **absolutely** important to be good in science and technology.
對國家而言，有傑出的科技是絕對重要的。

◇ It is **estimated** that the average life span of males in our country is 78.
據估計，我國男性的平均壽命是七十八歲。

◇ **Trillion** is a very large number. 兆是一個很大的數目。

◇ Our **digestion** system is quite complicated. 我們的消化系統是很複雜的。

◇ Exceedingly hot weather is **harmful** to us. 過熱的天氣對我們是有害的。

◇ He died by being **poisoned**. 他因中毒而死。

◇ Many busy people got **ulcer**. 很多忙人得到胃潰瘍。

◇ When you get **pneumonia**, you will have high fever. 你如得到肺炎，會發高燒。

◇ **Meningitis** will make you talk nonsense. 腦膜炎會使你語無倫次。

◇ **Strep throat** can be easily cured. 咽喉炎很容易醫治。

◇ This disease is not **fatal**. 這個病不是致命的。

Translate the following sentences into Chinese

1 It is absolutely necessary to be rigorous when we try to prove mathematical theorems. ↩

2 It is estimated that the average temperature in some areas of the earth is very high. ↩

3 There are trillions of cells in our body. ↩

4 We become sick when our digestion system does not function normally. ↩

5 Working too hard is harmful to us. ↩

6 Some poisoned food has bad smell. ↩

7 Scientists found out that some bacteria cause ulcer. ↩

8 It is dangerous for an old person to get pneumonia. ↩

9 It is not easy to detect meningitis. ↩

10 Strep throat can be easily detected. ↩

11 Most diseases are not fatal. ↩

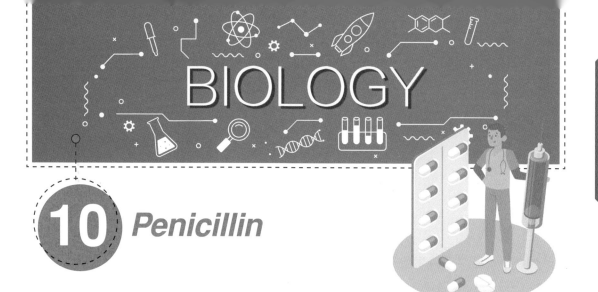

10 *Penicillin*

The German scientist, Paul Ehrlich, in 1909, was the first person who discovered that **chemicals** can be used to kill some bacteria without **side effects** on other cells. He found a chemical which can **cure** the **syphilis** disease. This chemical drug can be considered as the first **antibiotics**. Later, many antibiotics were found by American scientist Selman Waksman. The Scottish scientist Alexander Fleming **accidentally** found that certain **fungus** could kill some bacteria. With the help of drug companies, **penicillin** was **available** for human beings to **treat infections due to wounds effectively**.

德國科學家保羅‧埃爾利希在1909年首先發現可以用化學品殺死細菌，而且不會對其他的細胞有不良的副作用。他發現一種化學藥品可以治療梅毒，這種藥被認為是第一個抗生素。後來美國的科學家賽爾曼‧A‧瓦克斯曼發現了很多不同的抗生素。蘇格蘭科學家亞歷山大‧弗萊明在無意中發現某種黴菌可以殺死細菌。經由藥廠的幫助，盤尼西林因此問世。盤尼西林可以有效地醫治因細菌在傷口上所造成的感染。

Vocabulary

chemical (n.) 化學品
side effect 副作用
cure (v.) 治療
syphilis (n.) 梅毒
antibiotic (n.) 抗生素
accidentally (ad.) 意外地；偶然地
fungus (n.) 黴菌 (複數型：fungi)

penicillin (n.) 盤尼西林
available (a.) 可得到的
treat (v.) 醫療；治療
infection (n.) 感染；傳染
due to 由於
wound (n.) 傷口
effectively (ad.) 有效地

◇ Semiconductor industry uses a large number of special **chemicals**.
半導體工業大量使用特用化學品。

◇ We should be careful of **side effects** of drugs.　我們應該小心藥品的副作用。

◇ **Syphilis** is a horrible disease.　梅毒是一種可怕的病。

◇ **Antibiotics** are used extensively now.　抗生素現在已被普遍地使用。

◇ Many scientific achievements were discovered **accidentally**.
很多科學成果是在無意中發現的。

◇ Mushroom is a kind of **fungus**.　蘑菇是一種黴菌。

◇ Antibiotics are now **available** to the whole world.　抗生素現在全世界都可以得到。

◇ Doctors often **treat** patients by using antibiotics.　醫生常用抗生素醫治病人。

◇ Some **infections** can be cured without using any drug.　有些感染不用藥也可以醫治好。

◇ **Due to** illness, he cannot go to work.　由於生病，他無法上班工作。

◇ During a war, many soldiers die because of **wounds**.　在戰爭中，很多士兵因傷而死亡。

◇ **Penicillin** is very **effective** to cure many diseases.　盤尼西林對醫治很多疾病都很有效。

Translate the following sentences into Chinese

1 Special chemicals are important to our industry.

✍ ....

2 Drugs always have some kind of side effects.

✍ ....

3 Antibiotics cure many diseases.

✍ ....

4 Syphilis can be cured now.

✍ ....

5   Antibiotics are used extensively now.

    ....

6   There was a horrible car accident last night.

    ....

7   Some fungi are harmful to human beings.

    ....

8   We should thank scientists who discovered antibiotics.

    ....

9   Some people are allergic to antibiotics.

    ....

10 If one is weak, any infection will make him ill.

    ....

11 Due to diarrhea, he has to stay home.

    ....

12 If he has wounds, we should not let germs get into his body.

    ....

13 Penicillin is now used to dilute blood.

    ....

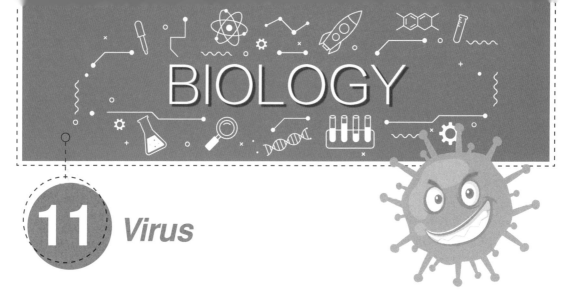

BIOLOGY

11 Virus

In the early days, scientists **realized** that there must be something smaller than bacteria and cannot be **detected** by using microscope at that time. The French biologist Charles Chamberland invented a **filter** which can **collect** bacteria in 1884. This filter was called Chamberland filter. People could then use the Chamberland filter to **remove** bacteria. In 1892, Russian scientist Dmitry Ivanosvsky removed bacteria from **tobacco** leaf **extracts**. He found that these extracts were still infectious. He did not know exactly why this was so. Six years later, Dutch scientist Martinus Beijerinck found out that some **agent** which passed through the filter **caused** the infection. He further observed that this agent **relies on** cells which are dividing. **Virus** was thus named.

在從前，科學家知道一定有東西比細菌還要小，並且無法由顯微鏡偵察到。法國生物學家查理斯‧尚柏朗在1884年發明了一種過濾器可以採集細菌，這種過濾器被稱為尚柏朗過濾器。如此人們就能用這種過濾器來去除細菌。在1892年，俄國科學家德米特里‧伊凡諾夫斯基將菸草葉萃取物上的細菌去除以後，發現這種菸草葉子物質仍然有傳染性。他不知道這是怎麼回事。六年之後，荷蘭科學家馬丁努斯‧威廉‧拜耶林克發現是某種化學藥劑穿過過濾器造成傳染。他進一步觀察發現，這種化學藥劑是依靠正在分裂中的細胞。病毒便從此被命名。

Vocabulary

realize (v.) 知道；理解	remove (v.) 除掉	cause (v.) 造成
detect (v.) 偵察；發現	tobacco (n.) 菸草	rely on 依靠
filter (n.) 過濾器	extract (n.) 萃取物質	virus (n.) 病毒
collect (v.) 蒐集	agent (n.) 化學品；劑	

Sentences

◇ It is hard for someone to **realize** that he is ignorant. 有的人不能理解自己的無知。

◇ It is not easy to **detect** the existence of virus. 偵察病毒的存在是很難的。

◇ **Filters** are used in many branches of engineering. 很多種類的工程都用到了過濾器。

◇ It is interesting to **collect** data. 蒐集資料是很有趣的。

◇ We should **remove** bad bacteria from our environment.
我們應該從環境中除掉有害的細菌。

◇ We should avoid **tobaccos**. 我們應該避免菸草。

◇ Chemists like to use **extracts** to do experiments. 化學家喜歡利用萃取物質做實驗。

◇ This is a special **agent** produced in our laboratory.
這個特別的化學藥劑是我們實驗室所製成的。

◇ This disease was **caused** by virus. 這種病是由病毒造成的。

◇ Scientists **rely on** hard work to succeed. 科學家依靠努力工作才能成功。

◇ No drug can kill **virus**. 沒有可以殺死病毒的藥。

Translate the following sentences into Chinese

1 High school students all realize that plants have the ability to perform
photosynthesis.

2 It is not easy to detect the existence of toxin in our food.

3 Filters are used in electrical engineering to retain the signals which we want.

4 Collecting data is often the first step to make a conclusion.

5 Engineers always need to remove unwanted materials.

👉

....

6 We should avoid making conclusions without careful thinking.

👉

....

7 Chemists must be skillful to get the extracts they want.

👉

....

8 To produce semiconductors, we need many special chemical agents.

👉

....

9 Virus always needs other living organisms to survive.

👉

....

10 We rely on good education to survive in the society.

👉

....

11 Virus exists everywhere in the air. We need not be worried about them if we are strong enough.

👉

....

12 *Ulcer*

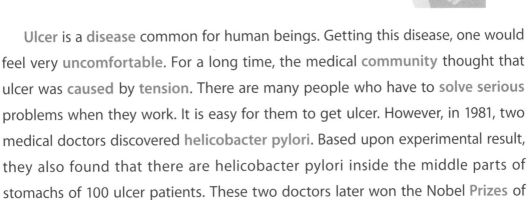

Ulcer is a disease common for human beings. Getting this disease, one would feel very uncomfortable. For a long time, the medical community thought that ulcer was caused by tension. There are many people who have to solve serious problems when they work. It is easy for them to get ulcer. However, in 1981, two medical doctors discovered helicobacter pylori. Based upon experimental result, they also found that there are helicobacter pylori inside the middle parts of stomachs of 100 ulcer patients. These two doctors later won the Nobel Prizes of Medical Science

胃潰瘍是人類常見的一種疾病，得了這種病的人會感到非常不舒服。有很長的時間，醫學界認為胃潰瘍是由於神經緊張所造成的。許多人工作的時候，必須解決嚴重的問題。這種人比較容易會得到胃潰瘍。可是，在1981年，有兩位醫生發現了幽門桿菌。根據實驗的結果，又發現100位得到胃潰瘍病人的胃中都有幽門桿菌。這兩位醫生後來得到了諾貝爾醫學獎。

Vocabulary

ulcer (n.) 胃潰瘍

disease (n.) 疾病

uncomfortable (a.) 不舒服的

community (n.) 團體；群體

cause (v.) 導致；造成

tension (n.) 緊張

solve (v.) 解決

serious (a.) 嚴重的

helicobacter pylori 幽門桿菌

prize (n.) 獎

◇ **Ulcer** is an annoying disease. 胃潰瘍是一個令人煩惱的疾病。

◇ Among all of the **diseases**, cancer is the most serious one.
在各種疾病中，癌症是最嚴重的。

◇ If you feel seriously **uncomfortable**, you should see a doctor immediately.
如果你感到嚴重地不舒服，你應該立刻看醫生。

◇ The academic **community** is always curious about new things.
學術團體總是對新事物有好奇心。

◇ Poverty **causes** illness. 貧窮會導致疾病。

◇ **Tension** in our daily life will cause a lot of troubles. 日常生活中的緊張會導致很多問題。

◇ Not everyone can **solve** difficult problems. 並非任何人都會解決難的問題。

◇ The problem of virus pandemic is quite **serious** now. 病毒疫情的問題目前很嚴重。

◇ He has won a lot of **prizes**. 他得了很多獎。

 Translate the following sentences into Chinese

1 Ulcer patients are usually well-educated people.

2 Mental disorder is a serious disease.

3 Every disease will make you uncomfortable.

4 The academic community is always interested in truth.

5 Many diseases are caused by bacteria.

6 We should avoid tension in our daily life.

7 We should try to calmly solve difficult problems.

8 The problem of locust in Africa is quite serious now.

9 It is by no means easy to win any Nobel Prize.

13 *Heart*

The **blood** in our bodies must be **circulating**. The circulation of blood depends upon heart and **vessel**. Inside the heart, there are **atrium** and **ventricle**. A heart will **contract** and **diastole**. When the heart contracts, blood will flow into the **artery**. When the heart diastoles, blood will return to the atrium. For an average person, the contraction and diastole will **take place roughly** seventy times every minute. Doctors often detect the number of our **heartbeats**. Actually they are detecting the function of our hearts. It is **abnormal** if the heartbeat is either too slow or too fast.

人體的血液必須循環，血液的流動要依靠心臟和血管。心臟裡面有心房和心室。心臟會有收縮和舒張的動作。當心臟收縮時，血液會進入動脈。當心臟舒張時，血液又會回到心房。一般人的收縮和舒張大約是每分鐘70次左右。醫生常常會偵測我們心跳的次數，其實就是在偵查我們心臟的功能。心跳太快或太慢都是不正常的。

Vocabulary

blood (n.) 血液

circulate (v.) 循環

vessel (n.) 血管

atrium (n.) 心房

ventricle (n.) 心室

contract (v.) 收縮

diastole (v.) 舒張

artery (n.) 動脈

take place 發生

roughly (ad.) 大約

heartbeat (n.) 心跳

abnormal (a.) 不正常的

◇ **Blood** is important for human beings. 血液對人類是很重要的。

◇ Blood is always **circulating** in our body. 血液一直在人體內循環。

◇ **Vessels** exist everywhere in our body. 血管遍布在人體內。

◇ Blood flows out from the **ventricle** into vessels. 血液從心室流出，進入血管。

◇ Blood flows into the **atrium**. 血液流入心房。

◇ The **contraction** and **diastole** of heart is critical to our life.
心臟的收縮和舒張對我們的生命極為重要。

◇ We must ensure that blood circulates smoothly in our **artery**.
我們一定要保持血液在動脈中順暢流通。

◇ We must not allow heart attack to **take place**. 我們一定不能讓心臟病發生。

◇ He is **roughly** 178 cm tall. 他的身高大約是 178 公分。

◇ His **heartbeat** is **abnormal**. 他的心跳不正常。

Translate the following sentences into Chinese

1 Health is important for human beings.

....

2 If blood stops circulating in our body, it would be disastrous.

....

3 Vessels are similar to roads which allow cars to move.

....

4 If the contraction and diastole of one's heart is abnormal, he should see a
doctor immediately.

....

5 We should try not to let pandemic take place.

....

6 He is roughly seventy years old.

....

7 He has an abnormal personality.

....

BIOLOGY

14 *Metabolism*

Metabolism is a chemical process in living organisms. We need energy to live. Eating food is a method to obtain energy and this is one function of metabolism. The body needs **protein** which is also obtained through a chemical process **transforming** food into protein. Another function of metabolism is to **get rid of wastes** in our body. If one does not have a normal metabolism, he will not be able to **consume** energy stored in the body. This is not good for the person.

新陳代謝是一種生物中的化學作用。我們需要熱量來維持生命，吃東西是一種取得熱量的方法，而這就是新陳代謝的一個功能。人體內的細胞需要蛋白質，這也是食物經由化學作用轉化而成的。新陳代謝的另一個作用是將體內的廢物去除。如果一個人新陳代謝的作用不夠好，會有熱量無法消耗的問題。這樣對這個人不太好。

Vocabulary

metabolism (n.) 新陳代謝

protein (n.) 蛋白質

transform (v.) 轉化

get rid of 去除

waste (n.) 廢物

consume (v.) 消耗

Sentences

◇ If our **metabolism** mechanism does not work well, we may become overweight.
若是新陳代謝失調，我們可能會過胖。

◇ There are a large number of different **proteins** in our body.
我們身體內有很多不同的蛋白質。

◇ The food which we eat will be **transformed** into different things through chemical processes in our body.
我們所吃的食物在我們體內會經由化學程序被轉化成不同的物質。

◇ Our body can **get rid of** things which we do not want to keep.
我們的身體可以去除不要的東西。

◇ It is inevitable that we will produce **wastes** in our body.
我們的身體不可避免產生廢物。

◇ We should **consume** energy in our body appropriately.
我們應適當地消耗體內的熱量。

Translate the following sentences into Chinese

1 Metabolism breaks down nutrients to produce energy.

   ∽

2 We are what our proteins are.

   ∽

3 Our body is able to use different chemical processes to transform the food we intake to different things we need.

   ∽

4 The mechanism to get rid of things which we do not want to keep is necessary for our health.

   ∽

5 We must be able to get rid of wastes in our body.

   ∽

6 It is not good for our health if we consume too much energy.

   ∽

15 Neuron

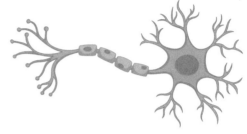

We can see and hear things because there is some kind of **stimulation** from the outside. We rely on **nerve** systems to be able to **respond** to the stimulations. Inside our body, there are cells which are called **neurons**. A neuron **consists of** a cell body and nerve **filaments**. The function of nerve filaments is to **transmit** the **signals** it receive to other neurons. There are roughly eight hundred billion neurons in our body.

我們能夠看得見、聽得見，都是因為外界對我們的人體有刺激。我們需要倚靠神經系統才能有所反應。人體內有一種細胞是神經細胞，神經細胞包含細胞本身和神經纖維。神經纖維的功能是將收到的訊號傳遞到別的神經細胞。人體中大約有8千億個神經細胞，遍布全部人體。

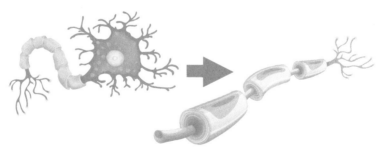

 Vocabulary

stimulation (n.) 刺激	consist of 包含
nerve (n.) 神經	filament (n.) 纖維
respond (v.) 反應	transmit (v.) 傳遞
neuron (n.) 神經細胞	signal (n.) 信號；訊號

Sentences

◇ Every living organism can respond to outside **stimulation**.
生物都會對外界刺激有所反應。

◇ If our **nerve** system is damaged, we will behave abnormally.
如果我們的神經系統受損，我們的行為就會不正常。

◇ If our nerve system does not work, we may not even be able to **respond** to light. 如果我們的神經系統不正常，我們可能連對光都無反應。

◇ **Neurons** are really amazing. 神經細胞實在很神奇。

◇ Our body **consists of** many different organs. Each of them performs a special function. 人體中包含了很多不同的器官，每個器官都有特定的功能。

◇ Nerve **filaments** spread all over our body. 神經纖維遍布全身。

◇ Signals are **transmitted** from our brain to organs of our body.
訊號從大腦傳遞到體內的器官。

◇ Our brain is sensitive to many **signals**. 大腦對很多訊號都很敏感。

Translate the following sentences into Chinese

1 As we grow older, our ability to respond to outside stimulations gets weaker.
....

2 We feel pain because a signal is received by our brain through our nerve system from some part of our body.
....

3 If our nerve system does not work, we may not be able to feel pain, which is not good.
....

4 Neurons form a network as they are connected to one another.
....

5 Living organism roughly consists of plants and animals.
....

6 We use nerve filaments to transmit signals to different parts of our body.
....

7 Signals inside our body are all electric signals.
....

16 *Reflection*

When we receive stimulations from the outside, we may respond immediately. For example, when our hands **touch** hot things, we will immediately **withdraw** our hands. This kind of **reaction** does not come from our brain and is a **reflection** through our **spine**. Good **athletes** almost rely on reflections **totally**. It is good that we human beings have spine because it will decrease the chances for us to get hurt. If our response to outside stimulations must go through our brain, we may be injured easily.

我們受到外界的刺激，立刻會有反應。比方說，手碰到熱的東西會立刻縮回。這種反應不經過大腦，而是經由脊椎所造成的反射動作。優秀的運動員幾乎是完全在依靠反射作用。人類有脊椎，乃是一件好事，它可以讓我們減少受傷害的機會。如果我們每次受到外來的刺激都要經過人腦才能做出反應，可能就會因此而受傷。

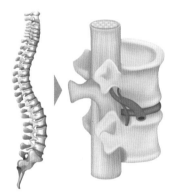

Vocabulary

touch (v.) 碰到

withdraw (v.) 縮回；抽回

reaction (n.) 反應

reflection (n.) 反射作用

spine (n.) 脊椎

athlete (n.) 運動員

totally (ad.) 完全地

Sentences

◇ Do not **touch** exceedingly hot things. 不要碰非常熱的東西。

◇ We **withdraw** hands or legs when we feel something wrong.
我們發現有問題時，會縮回手臂或腿。

◇ His **reaction** to this good news is joy. 他對這個好消息的反應是歡欣。

◇ It is lucky for us to be able to have the **reflection** mechanism.
我們有反射作用的功能是很幸運的。

◇ It is important to keep our **spine** straight. 保持脊椎筆直是很重要的。

◇ **Athletes** must be strong. 運動員一定要強壯。

◇ He is **totally** wrong. 他完全錯了。

Translate the following sentences into Chinese

1 Do not touch high-voltage electric wires. You may get hurt.

ᴄᴏ

2 If we cannot withdraw our hands immediately when we touch hot things, we may get hurt. ᴄᴏ

3 He has no visible reaction to this bad news.

ᴄᴏ

4 The reflection mechanism prevents us from getting hurt in many occasions.

ᴄᴏ

5 Not every animal has spine.

ᴄᴏ

6 Not everyone can become a good athlete.

ᴄᴏ

7 It is wrong to totally ignore the advice from scientists.

ᴄᴏ

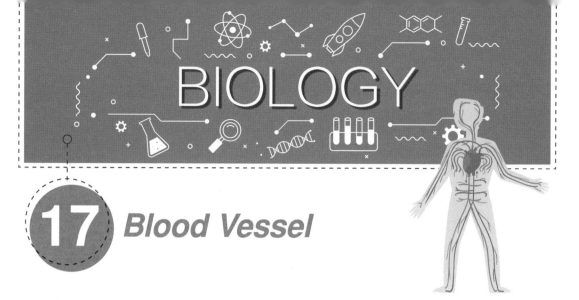

BIOLOGY

17 *Blood Vessel*

There are three kinds of **blood vessels**: **artery**, **vein** and **capillary**. When blood leaves the heart, it will first go to the artery. In other words, the artery is connected to the ventricle. As the heart contracts, blood flows into the artery. **Consequently**, the artery **expands**. The **pressure** onto the artery is called the **blood pressure**. The part of the artery close to the heart is bigger than that of the artery farther away from the heart. The blood in the artery will flow into capillary which exists all over the body. Finally, the blood in the capillaries will flow into the vein and get back to the heart.

　血管一共有三種：動脈、靜脈和微血管。血液離開心臟時，會先進入動脈；也就是說，動脈會和心室相接。心臟收縮時，血液會進入動脈，動脈會因此擴張，其所受到的壓力叫做血壓。和心臟離得較近的動脈血管比離較遠的粗。動脈的血液會流經微血管，微血管則遍布全身。微血管的血液最後會進入靜脈，再經由靜脈回到心臟。

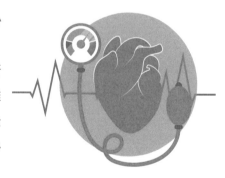

Vocabulary

blood vessel 血管	consequently (ad.) 因此
artery (n.) 動脈	expand (v.) 擴張
vein (n.) 靜脈	pressure (n.) 壓力
capillary (n.) 微血管	blood pressure 血壓

◇ We need **blood vessels** to transport oxygen to all of the body.
我們需要血管將氧氣傳送到全身。

◇ If your **artery** is blocked, you need to see a doctor. 動脈如果不通，必須要看醫生。

◇ **Veins** are thinner than arteries. 靜脈比動脈細。

◇ **Capillaries** are the smallest blood vessels in our body. 微血管是體內最小的血管。

◇ In winter, your blood vessels will contract. **Consequently** you need to be very careful. 冬天時血管會收縮，因此你必須非常小心。

◇ If one is very weak, his artery will not **expand** normally.
如果人身體很虛弱，動脈就不會正常地擴張。

◇ If one feels too much **pressure**, he may get sick. 如果人感到太大的壓力，可能會生病。

◇ High **blood pressure** is dangerous for you. 高血壓對你是很危險的。

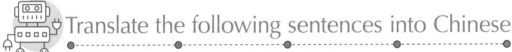
Translate the following sentences into Chinese

1 Blood vessels also transport nutrients to all of the body.

☙

2 If your artery is blocked, you may need to be installed a stent.

☙

3 Capillary wall lets nutrient pass through it.

☙

4 In hot weather, your blood vessels will not contract. Consequently you need not be worried about the high blood pressure problem.

☙

5 If your artery does not expand normally, you are actually sick.

☙

6 Everyone should know how to handle too much pressure in life.

☙

7 There are a lot of drugs which can help you reduce high blood pressure.

☙

BIOLOGY

18 *Food Digestion*

After eating, **nutrition** will be **absorbed** by our body. The food will first go through our **oral cavity**. The **saliva** inside our mouth will have some kind of chemical reaction with the food. Then the food goes into the **stomach** and has chemical reaction again with the **gastric fluid**. After this, it goes into the **small intestine**. The chemical process of **digestion** will take place in the front part of the small intestines and nutrients will be sent at the end part of small intestines into blood vessels so that the whole body may receive nutrients. Of course, some food cannot be digested. It goes into the **large intestine**. Large intestine will **discharge** all of the remaining waste out of the body through the **anus**.

　人吃了食物以後，養分會被人體吸收。食物首先通過口腔，口腔裡的唾液會對食物有化學作用。然後食物通過食道進入胃，胃中的胃液又再對食物進行消化作用。之後食物會進入小腸，在小腸的前段進行消化的化學作用，在小腸的後段將養分送到微血管。因此，人體的全身都會得到養分。當然還有一些食物是不能被分解的，它們就會進入大腸。大腸會將這些剩餘的殘渣經由肛門排出。

Vocabulary

nutrition (n.) 養分

absorb (v.) 吸收

oral cavity 口腔

saliva (n.) 唾液

stomach (n.) 胃

gastric fluid 胃液

small intestine 小腸

digestion (n.) 消化

large intestine 大腸

discharge (v.) 排出

anus (n.) 肛門

Sentences

◇ Poor people cannot gain enough **nutrition**. 窮人很難得到足夠的營養。

◇ Thin people cannot **absorb** nutrient. 瘦子很難吸收營養。

◇ We must keep our **oral cavity** clean. 我們一定要保持口腔清潔。

◇ We are lucky to have **saliva** in our mouth. 口內有唾液是一件幸運的事。

◇ Ulcer is a disease related to **stomach**. 胃潰瘍是一種與胃有關的疾病。

◇ If we get ulcer, we will feel the **gastric fluid**. 如果我們得了胃潰瘍，我們會感覺到胃液。

◇ The function of **small intestine** is related to **digestion**. 小腸的作用與消化有關。

◇ The function of **large intestine** is related to excreting. 大腸的作用與排泄有關。

◇ We have to be able to **discharge** waste. 我們要能排出廢物。

◇ Birds actually do not have **anuses**. 鳥類沒有肛門。

Translate the following sentences into Chinese

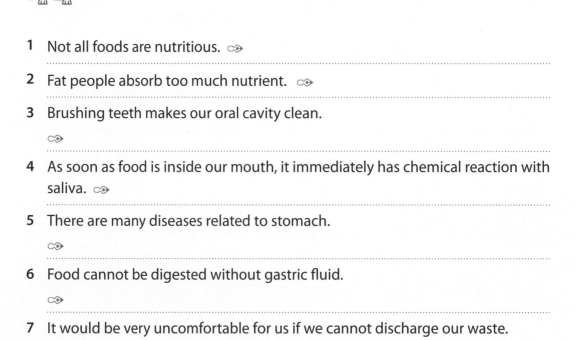

1 Not all foods are nutritious. ✑

2 Fat people absorb too much nutrient. ✑

3 Brushing teeth makes our oral cavity clean.
✑

4 As soon as food is inside our mouth, it immediately has chemical reaction with saliva. ✑

5 There are many diseases related to stomach.
✑

6 Food cannot be digested without gastric fluid.
✑

7 It would be very uncomfortable for us if we cannot discharge our waste.
✑

8 We have to keep our anus clean. ✑

19 Keeping Warm

The **temperature** of our body is kept as a **constant** under normal **conditions**. When it is cold outside, our brain will notice it and make vessels contract to **decrease** the consuming of energy. When the outside temperature gets higher, our body will be **sweating** to decrease body temperature. There are clever animals who will search for sunlight to **increase** body temperature or hide themselves in **cool** places to decrease body temperature. Some animals have very **thick** skin. **For example**, take a look at the **polar bears**. They are not afraid of **extremely** cold winter because of their thick **fur**.

人體的溫度在正常情況之下是保持不變的。當外界寒冷時，我們的腦部會知道，它會使得血管收縮，因而減少熱能的消耗。當外界溫度升高時，人體會出汗，這樣可以降低體溫。還有動物會聰明地尋找陽光來增加體溫，或是尋找陰涼的地方來降低體溫。有很多動物有相當厚的皮膚。舉例來說，看看北極熊，牠們的厚皮毛可以不怕極端寒冷的天氣。

Vocabulary

temperature (n.) 溫度

constant (n.) 不變；常數 / (a.) 不變的；固定的

condition (n.) 情況，條件

decrease (v.) 減少

sweat (v.) 出汗

increase (v.) 增加

cool (a.) 陰涼的

thick (a.) 厚的

for example 舉例來說

polar bear 北極熊

extremely (ad.) 極端地

fur (n.) 皮毛

Sentences

◇ Exceedingly high or low **temperature** is not good for your health.
溫度太高或太低對身體不好。

◇ In many precision instruments, temperature and pressure must be kept **constant**. 在很多精密設備的內部，溫度和壓力要保持不變。

◇ This result can be obtained only under certain **condition**.
這個結果只有在某種情況下才會出現。

◇ Your weight may **decrease** if you exercise more. 你如多運動，會減少體重。

◇ **Sweating** is necessary for you in hot weather. 大熱天，出汗是有其必要的。

◇ You should not allow your blood pressure to **increase** abnormally.
你不能讓血壓不正常地上升。

◇ You should always keep your temper **cool**. 你要永遠保持情緒冷靜。

◇ If it is cold, put on **thick** clothes. 如果天冷，穿上厚衣服。

◇ **For example**, you may get ill if you go to a very hot place.
舉例來說，你如果到很熱的地方，可能會生病。

◇ **Polar bears** can survive in exceedingly cold places. 北極熊可以在極冷的地方生存。

◇ Do not go **extreme**. 不要走極端。

◇ Many animals have very thick **fur** so that they are not afraid of cold weather.
很多動物有厚的毛皮，所以不怕冷天氣。

Translate the following sentences into Chinese

1 Presently, there are many machines which can keep temperature constant.

⇨ ....

2 In mathematics, constants are opposite to variables.

⇨ ....

3 This machine works well only under specific conditions.

⇨ ....

4 Your body temperature may decrease if you sweat.

⇨ ....

5   It is not good if your weight increases abnormally.

    ☞

6   Cool weather makes you feel comfortable.

    ☞

7   Thick clothes are necessary.

    ☞

8   For example, you may get ulcer if you work too hard.

    ☞

9   It is hard for polar bears to survive in the current condition.

    ☞

10 We must be alert to extreme weather.

    ☞

11 We are not encouraged to wear fur coats these days.

    ☞

BIOLOGY

20 Lung

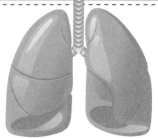

Many animals have **lungs**. The function of lung is to push oxygen into blood vessels and further into the heart. Besides, the lung can push **carbon dioxide** out of our body. Oxygen can be **combined** with other chemical compounds to generate energy. Without oxygen, there will be no activity in our body. **According to experience**, we will lose **sense** if we are in a **situation** of **lacking** of oxygen for two minutes. If the **duration** of lacking of oxygen is longer, our brain cells will stop functioning and we will be in **vegetative state**.

很多動物的體內都有肺。肺的功能是將氧氣送到血管,再到心臟。而且肺可以將二氧化碳排出體外。氧氣可以和體內其他的化合物結合,產生能量。如果我們在沒有氧氣的情況,人體內的所有活動都無法進行。根據經驗,人缺氧的時間超過2分鐘以後就會昏迷。缺氧的時間如果再長下去,腦細胞便會失去功能,而人會變成植物人。

Vocabulary

lung (n.) 肺
carbon dioxide 二氧化碳
combine (v.) 結合
according to 根據
experience (n.) 經驗
sense (n.) 意識;感覺;意義

situation (n.) 情況
lack (v.) 缺
duration (n.) 持續時間
vegetative (a.) 植物性的;植物人狀態的
state (n.) 狀態

Sentences

◇ If our **lung** does not function well, we will become very weak.
如果肺功能不彰，我們會變得很弱。

◇ We must discharge **carbon dioxide** to the air to be absorbed by plants.
二氧化碳必須排入空氣以被植物吸收。

◇ Many chemical compounds are **combined** in our body. 很多化合物在體內結合。

◇ **According to** experiments, there is a force between two objects.
根據實驗，兩個物體中有力存在。

◇ What he said makes no **sense** to me. 他說的話對我毫無意義。

◇ His **situation** is really bad. 他的情況的確很糟。

◇ He **lacks** exercises, so he is not strong. 他缺乏運動，所以他不強壯。

◇ The **duration** of his sleeping is getting shorter and shorter. 他睡覺的時間越來越短。

◇ When one person loses his sense and is still living, we say that he is in
vegetative state. 如果一個人失去了意識而仍活著，我們稱之為植物人。

◇ He is in the **state** of coma. 他在昏迷之中。

Translate the following sentences into Chinese

1 Our lung is important for our breathing.

✎

2 It is not good if the air is full of carbon dioxide.

✎

3 The combination process of chemical compounds in our body is very complicated.

✎

4 Many scientific discoveries are based upon experimental results.

✎

5 According to mathematics, his statement must be wrong.

✎

6 Common sense tells us that this is impossible.

✎
....

7 His situation is getting better and better.

✎
....

8 He lacks proper education.

✎
....

9 The duration of hot weather is really too long.

✎
....

10 He is in a state of great joy.

✎
....

PART 2

CHEMISTRY

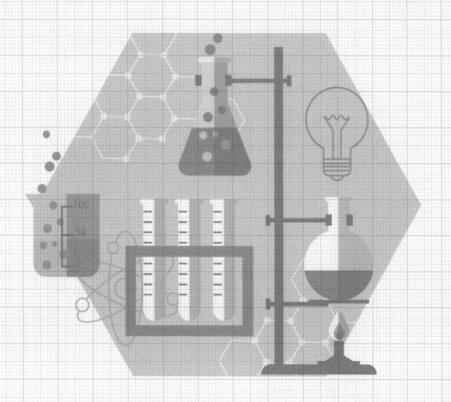

CHEMISTRY

 *Mixture*

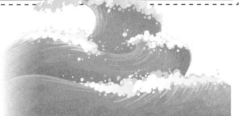

Most of the **substances** we see are **mixtures**. For example, seawater is a mixture, because through **exposure**, we can get **salt** from sea water. It can be seen that seawater is a mixture of salt and water. If the water we get is from **nature**, there will be **impurities**, which are not **suitable** for drinking. We can **remove** these impurities by **filtration**. So we know that water in nature is a mixture of water and some impurities.

我們常見的物質，大部分是混合物。比方說，海水就是混合物，因為經過曝曬，我們可以從海水中取得鹽，可見海水是鹽和水的混合物。若我們取得的水是來自自然界，那麼其中常會混有雜質，不適合飲用。我們可以用過濾的方法去掉這些雜質，所以我們可以得知自然界的水是水和一些雜質的混合物。

 Vocabulary

substance (n.) 物質

mixture (n.) 混合物

exposure (n.) 曝曬

salt (n.) 鹽

nature (n.) 自然界

impurity (n.) 雜質

suitable (a.) 適合

remove (v.) 去掉

filtration (n.) 過濾

Sentences

◇ This is a newly invented **substance**. 這是新發明的物質。

◇ Air is a **mixture**. 空氣是混合物。

◇ **Exposure** is a commonly used technology. 曝曬是一種常用的技術。

◇ We cannot live without **salt**. 我們不能缺鹽。

◇ We must respect **nature**. 我們一定要尊敬大自然。

◇ It is hard to obtain water without any **impurity**. 要得到完全沒有雜質的水是很困難的。

◇ This job is not **suitable** for you. 這個職務不適合你。

◇ Please **remove** the noise from the signal. 請將訊號中的雜訊去掉。

◇ Every chemical engineer knows **filtration**. 每一個化工工程師都知道過濾技術。

Translate the following sentences into Chinese

1 Most substances in nature are mixtures. ⌛

2 We must understand how nature works. ⌛

3 In every chemical product, impurities must be kept to the minimum.

⌛

4 Sometimes, we would remove air from a tube.

⌛

5 Many old people expose foods to sunlight to prepare meals.

⌛

6 Vegetables also contain salt. ⌛

7 It is hard to understand nature. ⌛

8 Impurity always exists in natural mixtures. ⌛

9 This school is suitable for you. ⌛

10 Noise can be removed by designing a good circuit.

⌛

CHEMISTRY

02 Element

Pure substances can be divided into two types: compounds and elements. Let's take water and salt as examples. Water can be broken down into two kinds of objects, namely hydrogen and oxygen, and salt can be broken down into sodium and chlorine, but we can no longer decompose hydrogen and oxygen by ordinary chemical methods, nor can we decompose sodium and chlorine. So we call these substances elements. You may not be satisfied with the definition we gave, because you don't understand what ordinary chemical methods are. Don't worry, in the following chapters, we will add other materials to make the definition of elements clearer.

純物質又可以分為兩種：化合物和元素。我們拿水和鹽來舉例，水可以分解成兩種物體，也就是氫和氧；食鹽可以被分解成鈉和氯。但是我們不能再用一般的化學方法將氫和氧分解了，也無法將鈉和氯再分解了，所以我們將這種物質叫做元素。同學們可能會對我們給的定義不滿意，因為你還不了解「一般化學方法」是什麼。別擔心，在後面的章節中，我們會再藉由其它資料的補充，讓大家對元素的定義更了解。

Vocabulary

pure (a.) 純的
compound (n.) 化合物
element (n.) 元素
salt (n.) 鹽
object (n.) 物體
hydrogen (n.) 氫
oxygen (n.) 氧

sodium (n.) 鈉
chlorine (v.) 氯
decompose (v.) 分解
satisfy (v.) 使……滿意 /
satisfied (a.) 感到滿意的
definition (n.) 定義
material (n.) 資料；材料；物質

 Sentences

◇ This water is not **pure**. 這水不純。

◇ Most drugs we take are **compounds**. 我們吃的藥大多都是化合物。

◇ **Elements** cannot be decomposed. 元素不能再被分解。

◇ All animals need **salt**. 所有動物都需要鹽。

◇ This is a strange **object**. 這是一個奇怪的物體。

◇ **Hydrogen** can be combined with oxygen to produce water.
氫可與氧結合產生水。

◇ Many chemical compounds can be **decomposed**. 很多化合物可被分解。

◇ I am not **satisfied** with your answer. 我不滿意你的回答 。

◇ The **definition** of this term is not clear. 這個術語的定義不明確。

◇ This is a rare **material**. 這是一種稀有物質。

 Translate the following sentences into Chinese

1 We can decompose a large problem into some small problems.

2 There is always a clear and precise definition for every mathematical term.

3 There is too much material in this book. Most students probably cannot digest it.

4 We require the chemical to be as pure as possible.

5 Are you satisfied with your present school?

6 Chemists must remember many compounds.

7 In the old days, it was hard to determine whether a material was a compound or an element.

CHEMISTRY

03 *Photosynthesis*

In 1774, the British scientist Priestley discovered **photosynthesis**. He found that the plant would **emit oxygen**. He also found that mice cannot **survive** for long in closed **spaces**, but if there are plants in the space, mice can survive longer. His other **experiment** was to put a plant in a glass bottle. A candle was placed in this bottle, and the candle was lit for a while and then **extinguished**. After twenty days, he lit the candle again with strong sunlight. Why was the candle lit again? The answer is because plants **produce** oxygen.

1774年，英國的科學家卜利士力發現了所謂的光合作用，也就是植物會釋放出氧氣。他同時也發現老鼠不能在密閉的空間中存活很久，但是如果空間中有植物，老鼠就可以存活更長的時間。他的另一個實驗是將一種植物放進了一個玻璃瓶，瓶內放入一支蠟燭，蠟燭點燃了一陣子後熄滅了。經過二十天以後，他用強烈的日光再度點燃了這支蠟燭。為什麼蠟燭又被點燃呢？答案是因為植物產生了氧氣的原因。

 Vocabulary

photosynthesis (n.) 光合作用

emit (v.) 放出；發出（光或氣體等）

oxygen (n.) 氧氣

survive (v.) 存活

space (n.) 空間

experiment (n.) 實驗

extinguish (v.) 熄滅

produce (v.) 產生

 Sentences

◇ Plants cannot live without **photosynthesis**.
植物如無光合作用，就無法生存。

◇ This process will **emit** a lot of odor. 這個步驟會釋放出很多氣味。

◇ There is not much **space** for us to play. 沒有多少空間可以給我們玩。

◇ Can we **survive** the war? 我們能在這場戰爭中存活嗎？

◇ This **experiment** is very important. 這個實驗很重要。

◇ The fire was finally **extinguished**. 火終於熄滅了。

◇ This car is **produced** in Taiwan. 這輛汽車是在台灣製造的。

◇ We cannot live without **oxygen**. 沒有氧氣，我們便無法存活。

 Translate the following sentences into Chinese

1 The fire emits a large amount of smoke.

☞
....

2 This experiment shows that our idea is feasible.

☞
....

3 It is hard to extinguish the raging fire.

☞
....

4 Trees emit a lot of oxygen.

☞
....

5 Taiwan is an important place to produce semiconductor products.

☞
....

6 This city is so crowded that there is no space for a large park. What a pity!

☞
....

7 No one can survive a nuclear war.

☞
....

CHEMISTRY

 **04** *Dalton's Atom Theory*

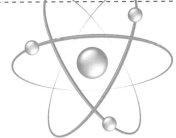

The British scientist Dalton **proposed** his **theory** of **atom**. Theories of Dalton **include** the following:

1. Elements are made of atoms.

2. Different elements are composed of different atoms, and different atoms have different **weights**.

3. The atoms in the same element are **identical**.

4. Atoms in one element can be used to synthesize compounds with atoms in other elements. The **ratio** of number of different atoms in the same compound is the same.

5. Atoms cannot be **manufactured**, cannot be **decomposed** further, and cannot be **destroyed** by chemical **reaction**. Chemical reactions only change the **relationship** between atoms.

英國科學家道耳吞提出了他的原子理論，道耳吞的理論包含以下幾點：

1.元素由原子所構成。

2.不同的元素由不同的原子所構成，不同的原子有不同的重量。

3.同一元素內的原子完全相同。

4.某元素內的原子可以和別的元素內的原子合成化合物。同一化合物內不同原子的數量比是相同的。

5.原子不能被製造，不能再被分解，也不可能被化學反應所破壞。化學反應僅僅改變原子和原子間的關係。

 Vocabulary

propose (v.) 提出，建議	weight (n.) 重量	decompose (v.) 分解
theory (n.) 理論	identical (a.) 同樣的	destroy (v.) 破壞
atom (n.) 原子	ratio (n.) 比；比率	reaction (n.) 反應
include (v.) 包含	manufacture (v.) 製造	relationship (n.) 關係

Sentences

◇ He **proposed** a new method to solve the problem.
他提出了一個新的方法來解決這個問題。

◇ Every **atom** is exceedingly small. 原子都非常小。

◇ It is hard to understand the **theory** of electromagnetics. 電磁學的理論是很難懂的。

◇ You should lose **weight**. 你應該減重。

◇ They are **identical**. 他們是相同的。

◇ The **ratio** of boys and girls in this school is 5:4. 這所學校男生和女生的比例是 5：4。

◇ It is hard to **manufacture** this machine. 製造這個機器是很困難的。

◇ We cannot **decompose** this substance any further. 我們不能進一步地分解這個物質。

◇ The house was **destroyed** by fire. 這座房子被火燒毀了。

◇ The **reaction** to my proposal is not very good. 我的提案反應不太好。

◇ The **relationship** between him and his father is always good.
他和他父親的關係一直很好。

Translate the following sentences into Chinese

1 It is hard to see an atom because it is too small.

2 I would like to decompose this problem into two small problems.

3 They are identical twins.

4 We cannot manufacture airplanes in our country.

5 He proposed a law which was opposed by a lot of people.

6 We study different chemical reactions in college.

7 He only knows theories and does not know engineering details.

8 We always tend to minimize the weight of a machine.

9 A good friendship cannot easily be destroyed.

05 More on Dalton's Atom Theory

Dalton's atom theory has great **contribution** to **science**. In the past we only knew that elements cannot be decomposed by **ordinary** chemical methods. Now we know that elements are single-atom substances. Water is not an element because there are hydrogen atoms and oxygen atoms in water, and oxygen is an element because there is only one kind of atom in oxygen. So now we can use this definition to **test whether** a substance is an element. The first four **statements** of Dalton's atom theory are correct, but the last one is wrong, because people later found that there are **electrons**, **protons** and **neutrons** in an atom.

　　道耳吞的原子說對人類科學的貢獻極大。過去我們只知道元素是不能用一般化學方法分解的，現在我們知道元素是單一原子的物質。水不是元素，因為水裡有氫原子和氧原子；而氧是元素，因為氧裡面只有一種原子。所以現在我們可以用這個定義來檢定一個物質是否為元素。道耳吞原子說的前四個陳述都是正確的，最後一點卻有誤，因為後人發現原子內還有電子、質子和中子。

Vocabulary

contribution (n.) 貢獻

science (n.) 科學

ordinary (a.) 一般的

test (v.) 檢定；檢測

whether (conj.) 是否

statement (n.) 說明；陳述

electron (n.) 電子

proton (n.) 質子

neutron (n.) 中子

Sentences

◇ He has great **contribution** to the mankind. 他對人類有很大的貢獻。

◇ We should always pay close attention to the definition of a term in **science**.
我們應該總是對科學術語的定義非常注意。

◇ He is an **ordinary** person. 他是一個普通的人。

◇ This equipment can be used to **test** whether this bottle contains hydrogen.
這個設備可以用來檢定瓶子內是否有氫氣。

◇ I do not know **whether** his statement is correct or not. 我不知道他的說法是否正確。

◇ His latest **statement** is quite significant. 他最新的聲明相當有意義。

◇ Electric current is a flow of **electrons**. 電流是電子的流動。

◇ **Protons** do not leave the atom. 質子不離開原子。

Translate the following sentences into Chinese

1 Everyone has some contribution to his country.

....

2 It is a bad habit to pay little attention to the definition of a term in science.

....

3 Electrons can move out of an atom while protons and neutrons cannot.

....

4 Advanced countries are usually good in science.

....

5 He barely makes any statement.

....

6 This equipment can be used to test whether the capacitor can endure large voltage.

....

7 I do not know whether the voltage is large enough.

....

CHEMISTRY

06 *Dalton*

It is **worth mentioning** that Dalton was a **Christian**, but belonged to the **Quaker sect**. This sect was **discriminated** against in Britain at that time. Therefore Dalton had no **formal** education. The Quaker Church **emphasized social justice**. They **opposed violence** and war, and they also opposed **slavery**. They believed that women and men had the same **rights**. Dalton's other contribution was about **color blindness**. This is why some people now call color blindness Daulton **syndrome**, just to **commemorate** him.

值得一提的是道耳吞是基督徒，但屬於桂格教派，這個教派當時在英國飽受歧視，因此道耳吞沒有接受過什麼正式的教育。桂格教會強調社會正義，他們反對暴力和戰爭，也反對奴隸制度，贊成女性和男性有同樣的權利。道耳吞的另一貢獻是關於色盲，所以現在有人將色盲稱之為道耳吞症侯群，就是為了紀念他。

 Vocabulary

worth (a.) 值得（做……）	social justice 社會正義
mention (v.) 提到；提及	oppose (v.) 反對
Christian (n.) 基督徒	violence (n.) 暴力
Quaker (n.) 桂格會教徒	slavery (n.) 奴隸制度
sect (n.) 教派；派別	right (n.) 權利
discriminate (v.) 歧視	color blindness 色盲
formal (a.) 正式的	syndrome (n.) 症侯群
emphasize (v.) 強調	commemorate (v.) 紀念

Sentences

◇ This book is **worth** reading. 這本書值得一讀。

◇ Did you **mention** your father? 你有提到你的爸爸嗎？

◇ A good **Christian** loves others. 好的基督教徒是愛人的。

◇ **Quakers** are peace-loving people. 桂格派教徒愛好和平。

◇ He belongs to a strange **sect**. 他屬於一個奇特的教派。

◇ We should never **discriminate** against any race. 我們不該歧視任何種族。

◇ Although he has never received **formal** education, he is still a brilliant scholar.
雖然他沒有受過正式的教育，他仍是一位傑出的學者。

◇ We must **emphasize** equality. 我們一定要強調平等。

◇ A country must have **social justice**. 國家一定要有社會正義。

◇ I strongly **oppose** the use of military force. 我強力反對使用武力。

◇ This country is full of **violence**. 這個國家充滿暴力。

◇ I am absolutely against **slavery**. 我堅決反對奴隸制度。

◇ You have the **right** to vote when you are eighteen years old.
你在十八歲以後就有選舉權。

◇ **Color blindness** is not a serious matter. 色盲不是嚴重的事。

◇ This special **syndrome** was discovered by a medical doctor.
這種特別的症侯群是一位醫生發現的。

◇ This holiday is to **commemorate** a great mathematician.
這個假日是為了紀念一位偉大的數學家。

Translate the following sentences into Chinese

1 America is a Christian country.

✐ ....

2 Color blindness is not common.

✐ ....

3 This stamp is to commemorate the person who founded our country.

✐ ....

4 We should never discriminate against any religion.

⟳

....

5 We seldom emphasize equality now.

⟳

....

6 Formal education is not important to some people.

⟳

....

7 No justice is without forgiveness.

⟳

....

8 Did you mention your experiment to your teacher?

⟳

....

9 I strongly oppose the law because it is against social justice.

⟳

....

10 Use your rights wisely.

⟳

....

11 It is hard to understand why slavery existed in America for so long.

⟳

....

12 A country without social justice cannot be a peaceful country.

⟳

....

13 It is hard to detect this syndrome.

⟳

....

14 No problem can be solved by violence.

⟳

....

15 This problem is not worth mentioning.

⟳

....

CHEMISTRY

07 *Avogadro*

Avogadro was born in an **aristocratic family** in Italy. He had a **brilliant** career in the **legal profession**, but he was also **passionate** about natural science and mathematics. In 1811, he said that the most elementary items in a gas are not necessarily atoms, but may be **molecules composed** of atoms. We can say that Avogadro was the first person who had a **definite concept** of "molecule." His greatest **contribution** to chemistry was his Avogadro **hypothesis**.

　　亞佛加厥出身於義大利的貴族世家。他在法律專業的事業非常傑出,但他卻同時熱衷於自然科學和數學的研究。在1811年,他說「氣體內最基本的個體,不一定是原子,而可能是由原子集合而成的分子。」我們可以說亞佛加厥是第一個對「分子」有明確觀念的人。他對化學的最大貢獻,乃是他所提出的亞佛加厥假說。

Vocabulary

aristocratic (a.) 貴族的

aristocratic family 世家

brilliant (a.) 傑出的

legal (a.) 法律的;合法的

profession (n.) 專業;事業

passionate (a.) 熱衷的

molecule (n.) 分子

compose (v.) 集合;組成

definite (a.) 確定的;明確的

concept (n.) 觀念

contribution (n.) 貢獻

hypothesis (n.) 假說

Sentences

◇ He has an **aristocratic** manner. 他有貴族的氣質。

◇ He is **brilliant** in mathematics. 他在數學上表現很傑山。

◇ His action is **legal**. 他的行為是合法的。

◇ He is good in his **profession**. 他在他的專業表現良好。

◇ He is **passionate** about playing violin. 他熱衷於拉小提琴。

◇ A **molecule** is composed of atoms. 分子是由原子組成的。

◇ The Chinese is **composed** of many races. 中國人是很多種族集合而成。

◇ He did not give me a **definite** answer. 他沒有給我一個確定的答案。

◇ We must have a clear **concept** of what we talk about.
我們對自己的談話必須有清楚的概念。

◇ He has great **contribution** to science. 他對科學有很大的貢獻。

◇ This **hypothesis** is accepted by the science community.
這個假說是科學界所接受的。

Translate the following sentences into Chinese

1 He has an aristocratic ancestor.

☞

....

2 He is brilliant in music and literature.

☞

....

3 The air is composed of hydrogen and oxygen.

☞

....

4 We must have a clear concept of basic science.

☞

....

5 He has great contribution to history of China.

....

6 He always gives definite answers.

....

7 This is only a hypothesis.

....

8 Every action of the President must be legal.

....

9 This machine is composed of a large number of components.

....

10 He is passionate about medical science.

....

11 He is in the computer science profession.

....

CHEMISTRY

08 *Thomson*

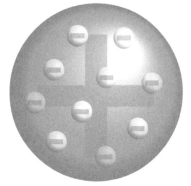

J. J. Thomson was a British scientist. He **confirmed** the **existence** of **electrons** and he **proposed** an atomic **model**. In this model, the positive charges in the atom are like a "soup" or a cloud. The electrons which are negatively charged spread all over the atom, like the **raisins** inside a **pudding**. This model **explains** why an atom is not electrically charged because the positive and negative charges **cancel** each other. Thomson **mentioned** neither **proton** nor **nucleus** which were discovered by Rutherford later. Rutherford **conducted** an experiment in which he **emitted** positively charged **particles** onto a **gold foil**. If Thomson's atomic model were correct, all of the particles will pass through the foil. Yet, the experiment showed that while most particles went through, a small amount of particles **reflected** back. Therefore, Rutherford proposed that there must be a nucleus and some particles which are positively charged.

約瑟夫·湯姆森是英國的科學家。他確認了電子的存在,也提出了一個原子模型。在這個模型中,原子內部充滿了正電,就像一碗「湯」或一朵雲;帶有負電的電子散布在原子中,就像布丁中含有葡萄乾。這個模型說明了為何原子是不帶電的,因為內部的正電和負電互相抵消。湯姆森沒有提到質子和原子核,質子和原子核是由拉塞福後來所發現的。拉塞福進行了一個實驗,他將帶有正電的粒子射往一個金箔。如果湯姆森的原子模型是正確的,所有的粒子應該都可以穿透金箔。但是實驗顯示,絕大多數的粒子的確是穿透金箔的,但有一些粒子卻反射回來。因此,拉塞福確定原子內有一個原子核,而且有粒子是帶正電的。

Vocabulary

confirm (v.) 確認

existence (n.) 存在

electron (n.) 電子

propose (v.) 建議；提出

model (n.) 模型

raisin (n.) 葡萄乾

pudding (n.) 布丁

explain (v.) 說明；解釋

cancel (v.) 取消；抵消

mention (v.) 提到；提及

proton (n.) 質子

nucleus (n.) 原子核

conduct (v.) 進行

emit (v.) 射出

particle (n.) 粒子

gold (n.) 金 / (a.) 含金的

foil (n.) 箔

reflect (v.) 反射

Sentences

◇ This experiment **confirmed** the correctness of his hypothesis.
這個實驗確認了他的假設的正確性。

◇ The discovery of the **existence** of proton was important to science.
發現質子的存在對科學是重要的。

◇ The **electron** microscope uses an electron beam. 電子顯微鏡利用了電子束。

◇ He **proposed** to repeat the experiment. 他提議再做一次這個實驗。

◇ No one can propose a **model** of the universe. 沒有人能提出宇宙的模型。

◇ Many cakes have **raisins**. 很多蛋糕裡有葡萄乾。

◇ **Pudding** is always delicious. 布丁總是美味的。

◇ Can you **explain** this theory clearly? 你能清楚地說明這個理論嗎？

◇ These two opposite forces may **cancel** each other. 這兩個相反的力可能會互相抵消。

◇ He **mentioned** his method to solve this mathematical problem in his latest published paper. 他在他最近發表的論文中提到解這道數學題的方法。

◇ **Protons** do not move out of the atom. 質子不離開原子。

◇ The **nucleus** of an atom contains protons and neutrons. 原子核內有質子和中子。

◇ Faraday **conducted** a large number of experiments. 法拉第做過大量的實驗。

◇ Thomson's experiment involved the **emitting** of charged **particles**.
湯姆森的實驗牽涉到帶電粒子的射出。

◇ **Gold** is a precious metal. 金子是貴重的金屬。

◇ Industry uses **foil** extensively. 工業界普遍地使用箔片。

◇ Light can be **reflected** so that we can see things. 光會反射，所以我們可以看見東西。

Translate the following sentences into Chinese

1 This experiment confirmed that oxygen is critical to life.

....

2 The discovery of hydrogen was really marvelous.

....

3 The electron beam of an electron microscope must be very narrow.

....

4 He proposed to import the semiconductor technology.

....

5 It is important to know the model of a transistor before we can use it.

....

6 Can you explain why this circuit works?

....

7 The concert is canceled.

....

8 He seldom mentions his achievements.

☞

....

9 No one knows why protons are positively charged.

☞

....

10 The nucleus of an atom is exceedingly small.

☞

....

11 Scientists rely on experiments.

☞

....

12 Many sophisticated instruments involve the emitting of charged particles.

☞

....

13 Gold is not easy to be oxidized.

☞

....

14 It would be interesting to imagine what happens if light cannot be reflected.

☞

....

09 Rutherford's Atomic Model

Rutherford conducted a very famous gold foil experiment. Based on the experimental results, Rutherford confirmed that a particle which exists in every atom is positively charged and can be named as proton. This is how protons were discovered.

Up to the present, we may have the following conclusion.

1. There are negatively charged electrons in an atom.

2. There are positively charged protons in the nucleus.

3. The number of electrons and the number of protons are equal.

4. The electrons surround the nucleus and are outside of the nucleus.

5. The electrons revolve around the nucleus with high speed and in fixed orbits.

The Rutherford's atomic model was a significant one in science because it clearly mentioned nucleus and proton. Yet it was hard to explain why the electrons which are negatively charged would not be attracted by the positively protons.

拉塞福做了一個著名的金箔實驗。根據實驗結果，拉塞福認定一種原子內都有的粒子，帶有正電，可以命名為質子。質子就是如此被發現的。

到目前為止，我們可以有以下的結論：

1.原子中有帶有負電的電子。

2.原子核中有帶有正電的質子。

3.電子的數目和質子的數目是相等的。

4.電子圍繞著原子核，在原子核的外圍。

5.電子圍繞著原子核旋轉，速度很快且軌道固定。

　　拉塞福的原子模型是科學的一個重要里程碑，因為他很清楚地提到原子核和質子。但是這個模型無法解釋帶有負電的電子為何不被帶有正電的質子吸引。

Vocabulary

based on　根據	speed (n.) 速度
conclusion (n.) 結論	fixed (a.) 固定的
negatively charged　帶有負電	orbit (n.) 軌道
positively charged　帶有正電	significant (a.) 有重大意義的
surround (v.) 繞著；圍繞	explain (v.) 解釋
revolve (v.) 旋轉	attract (v.) 吸引

Sentences

◇ His conclusion is **based on** his experimental results. 他的結論是根據他的實驗結果。

◇ His **conclusion** is not correct. 他的結論不正確。

◇ Electrons are **negatively charged**. 電子帶負電。

◇ His house is **surrounded** by trees. 他的房子周圍都是樹。

◇ The earth **revolves** around the sun. 地球圍繞著太陽旋轉。

◇ The **speed** of an airplane is larger than that of a train. 飛機的速度大過火車的速度。

◇ The moon revolves around the earth in a **fixed orbit**. 月亮圍繞地球轉的軌道是固定的。

◇ The discovery of oxygen is a **significant** event in the history of science.
發現氧是科學史上的重大事件。

◇ It is hard to **explain** the relativity theory. 相對論是很難解釋的。

◇ Positive and negative electric charges **attract** each other. 正負電荷互相吸引。

1 No definite conclusion can be made based on his experimental results.

2 He is always very careful when he makes a conclusion.

3 He discovered that everything contains atoms.

4 Electrons flow in the electric current.

5 Every island is surrounded by oceans.

6 Many stars revolve around the sun.

7 It is amazing that the high speed train can be so stable.

8 Some satellites revolve around the earth in fixed orbits.

9 His thesis is quite significant.

10 It is hard to explain many difficult scientific theories.

11 His hypothesis is quite attractive to many scientists.

CHEMISTRY

10 *Moseley*

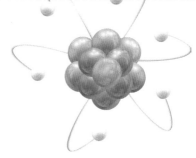

The reader certainly would like to know the number of electrons in the atom. In 1911, Dutch scientist Antonius van den Broek proposed a **theory** that the **atomic number** is the number of electrons, but he could not **prove** it. In 1913, British scientist Henry Moseley used **cathode rays** to **strike metal** to **generate X-rays**, and found that the larger the atomic number, the higher the **frequency** of X-rays. His experiment was quite **complicated**, and finally he got an **extremely** important **conclusion**. The atomic number of an element is the number of protons of that atom. Because the number of protons is equal to the number of electrons, the atomic order is also the number of electrons.

Henry Moseley was so **outstanding**. Why didn't he win the **Nobel Prize**? In 1915, when World War I broke out, Moseley joined the **army** and died in **Turkey** (**Ottoman Empire** at the time) at the age of 27. Since then, the British government has not **accepted** outstanding scientists into the army.

讀者一定想知道原子中的電子數目。1911年,荷蘭科學家安東尼斯・范・登・布羅克提出一種理論:原子序是電子的數目,但他無法證明。1913年英國科學家亨利・莫色勒利用陰極射線撞擊金屬產生X射線,發現原子序越大,X射線的頻率就越高。他的實驗相當複雜,最後使他得到了一個極重要的結論:某元素的原子序是該原子的質子數目,因為質子數目等於電子數目,原子序也是電子數目。

莫色勒如此傑出,為何他沒有得到諾貝爾獎?1915年,一次世界大戰爆發,莫色勒從軍,死於土耳其(當時是奧圖曼帝國),得年27歲。從此以後,英國政府不接受傑出科學家從軍。

Vocabulary

theory (n.) 理論	complicated (a.) 複雜的
atomic number 原子序	extremely (ad.) 極度地
prove (v.) 證明	conclusion (n.) 結論
cathode (n.) 陰極	outstanding (a.) 傑出的
ray (n.) 射線	prize (n.) 獎
cathode ray 陰極射線	Nobel Prize 諾貝爾獎
strike (v.) 撞擊	army (n.) 陸軍；軍人
metal (n.) 金屬	Turkey (n.) 土耳其
generate (v.) 產生	empire (n.) 帝國
X-ray X射線	Ottoman Empire 奧圖曼帝國
frequency (n.) 頻率	accept (v.) 接受

Sentences

◇ This **theory** is very **complicated**. 這個理論相當複雜。

◇ You can find the **atomic number** of any element in the periodic table.
你可以在週期表內找到任一元素的原子序。

◇ I cannot **prove** this theorem. 我無法證明這個定理。

◇ The **cathode rays** were used in many significant experiments.
陰極射線被用在很多重要的實驗中。

◇ Many scientists **strike** a metal with particles. 很多科學家用粒子撞擊金屬。

◇ **Metal** is hard. 金屬是硬的。

◇ Plants **generate** oxygen through photosynthesis. 植物經由光合作用產生氧氣。

◇ If a signal oscillates 100 times per second, its **frequency** is 100.
如果一個訊號在一秒鐘內震動一百次，它的頻率就是 100。

◇ **X-ray** is used in many hospitals now. 現在很多醫院會使用 X 光。

◇ This is an **extremely** significant discovery. 這是一個極為重要的發現。

◇ We have to perform many experiments before we reach the **conclusion**.
下結論以前，我們必須做很多實驗。

◇ He is an **outstanding** scientist. 他是個傑出的科學家。

◇ He has won a lot of prestigious **prizes**. 他得過很多有名望的獎。

◇ He is a **Nobel Prize** winner. 他得過諾貝爾獎。

◇ Have you ever joined the **army**? 你有當過兵嗎？

◇ The territory of **Turkey** spreads across both Europe and Asia.
土耳其的領土橫跨歐亞兩洲。

◇ Britain was a large **empire** before. 英國過去是一個龐大的帝國。

◇ **Ottoman Empire** was very large before. 奧圖曼帝國過去很大。

◇ I cannot **accept** his idea. 我不能接受他的想法。

 Translate the following sentences into Chinese

1 One has to be very rigorous when he proves a mathematical theorem.

↷

2 This is only a theory.

↷

3 I cannot memorize the atomic numbers of all elements.

↷

4 The cathode rays were used in TV for a while.

↷

5 Many instruments involve the striking of particles.

↷

6 Metal is used extensively in industries.

↷

7 It is important to be able to generate electricity.

☞ ....

8 X-ray machines are hard to produce.

☞ ....

9 It is hard to deal with high frequency signals.

☞ ....

10 This new discovery is significant.

☞ ....

11 He made a wrong conclusion.

☞ ....

12 His research is outstanding.

☞ ....

13 He has never won any prize.

☞ ....

14 It is difficult to be a Nobel Prize winner.

☞ ....

15 I have joined the army.

☞ ....

16 I accepted his proposal.

☞ ....

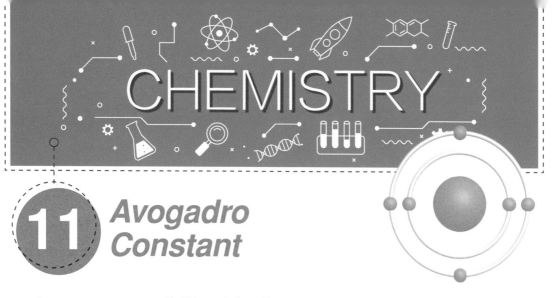

CHEMISTRY

11 Avogadro Constant

Atoms are very small. We can hardly **measure** the **mass** of an atom. Yet we can decide the **relative** mass of the atom of an element. Let us use **carbon** as our **standard**. There are six protons and six **neutrons** in an atom of carbon. Therefore scientists **determined** the atomic weight of carbon to be 12. Having the atomic weight of carbon, we can determine the atomic weight of oxygen to be 16. There is another problem. Suppose we have one gram of carbon. How many atoms are there? This is indeed a problem which is not easy to get an answer, but the Italian scientist Avogadro got an answer. He knew that the atomic weight of carbon is 12. He concluded that there are 6×10^{23} atoms in 12 grams of carbon. This was a great discovery. To **commemorate** him, 6×10^{23} is called the Avogadro **Constant**.

原子是非常小的東西，我們幾乎不可能測量出一個原子的質量。可是我們可以用一種相對的方法來表示元素原子的質量。以碳作為標準，碳原子有6個質子和6個中子，因此科學家認定碳的原子量是12。有了碳的原子量，我們可以確定氧的原子量是16。還有一個問題，假設我們有1公克的碳，這些碳裡面究竟有多少原子？這實在是一個很不容易得到答案的問題，可是義大利科學家亞佛加厥得到了一個答案。他知道碳的原子量是12，他算出12公克的碳有6×10^{23}個碳原子。這是一個非常偉大的發現，為了紀念他，6×10^{23}被稱為亞佛加厥常數。

Vocabulary

measure (v.) 測量	carbon (n.) 碳	determine (v.) 決定；確定
mass (n.) 質量	standard (n.) 標準	commemorate (v.) 紀念
relative (a.) 相對的	neutron (n.) 中子	constant (n.) 常數

 Sentences

◇ It is difficult to **measure** the speed of light. 測量光速是很難的。

◇ The **mass** of an object is different from the weight of an object.
一個物體的質量和重量是不同的。

◇ As compared with his classmates, he is **relatively** tall.
相對於他的同班同學,他是高的。

◇ **Carbon** atoms exist in many compounds. 碳原子存在於各種化合物中。

◇ There are many **standards** in the communication community. 通訊界有很多標準。

◇ **Neutrons** are not electrically charged. 中子不帶電。

◇ I **determined** to be an electrical engineer when I was in high school.
我在高中時決定要當電子工程師。

◇ The name of this university is to **commemorate** a great scientist.
這所大學的名字是為了紀念一位偉大的科學家。

◇ **Constants** in mathematics are opposite to variables. 數學裡的常數和變數相反。

 Translate the following sentences into Chinese

1 It is difficult to measure the mass of the earth.

....

2 The mass of an object remains the same as the object is moved to the moon.

....

3 When you study physics, you will find that relativity is an important concept.

....

4 Organic compounds contain carbon atoms.

....

5 It is good to have many industrial standards.

6 It is hard to understand neutrons.

7 He determined to devote himself to scientific research.

8 This song was written to commemorate all of the soldiers who had died in the war.

9 Constants in mathematics will not be changed.

CHEMISTRY

12 States of Material

Some material has **fixed volume** and **shape**. These **characteristics** will not be changed by using different **containers**. We say that these materials are in the **solid** state. Wood and **steel** are such material. **So far as water is concerned**, although its volume is fixed, its shape will change as the shape of its container changes. This kind of material is in the **liquid** state. We can **compress** air. Thus air is in the **gaseous** state. The state of materials can change with **environment**. For example, water may become ice as the temperature drops. Its state changes from liquid to solid. We can also heat the water so that it is transformed into **vapor**. Its state is changed from liquid to gaseous.

有些物質有固定的體積和形狀，這些性質不會因容器不同而改變。這種物質的狀態是固態，木材和鋼鐵等都是這種物質。對水而言，雖然水的體積固定，但是形狀可以隨容器而改變，這種物質的狀態是液態。我們可以壓縮空氣，所以空氣的狀態是氣態。物質的狀態可以隨環境而改變。比方說，水可以因為溫度降低而變成冰，狀態由液態變成固態。我們也可以將水加熱變成水蒸氣，狀態由液態變成氣態。

Vocabulary

fixed (a.) 固定的
volume (n.) 體積
shape (n.) 形狀
characteristics (n.) 性質；特徵
container (n.) 容器
solid (a.) 固體的
steel (n.) 鋼鐵

so far as . . . is concerned 就……而言
liquid (a.) 液體的
compress (v.) 壓縮
gaseous (a.) 氣體的
environment (n.) 環境
vapor (n.) 水蒸氣

Sentences

◇ The temperature in many factories is **fixed**. 在很多工廠裡，溫度是固定的。

◇ **Volume** is an important parameter in physics. 體積在物理上是一個重要的參數。

◇ This vase has an elegant **shape**. 這個瓶子有一個優雅的形狀。

◇ We must pay attention to critical **characteristics** of a compound.
我們必須注意化合物的關鍵性性質。

◇ **Containers** used in industry are often customized. 工業用容器往往是客製化的。

◇ Metals are all in **solid** state in room temperature. 金屬在室溫中都是固體。

◇ There are different kinds of **steels**. 鋼鐵有許多種。

◇ **So far as** relativity theory **is concerned**, only a few people understand it.
就相對論而言，很少人懂它。

◇ Seriously sick people rely on **liquid** to live. 重病者靠液體維生。

◇ **Compressors** are widely used in industry. 工業界常用壓縮機。

◇ If a substance is in **gaseous** state, it can be invisible.
如果物質是氣體，它可能是看不見的。

◇ It is important to keep our **environment** clean. 保持環境乾淨是很重要的。

◇ **Vapor** was an important source of energy in the old days.
在過去，水蒸氣是一種重要的能源。

Translate the following sentences into Chinese

1 The pressure in an airplane is always fixed.

　↩

....

2 Volume and pressure were mentioned in Boyle's Law.

　↩

....

3 Sports cars all have handsome shapes.

　↩

....

4 We must pay attention to our health.

　↩

....

5 Some special containers used in industry are very expensive.

↩

....

6 Do you know why gold is the most expensive metal?

↩

....

7 There are different kinds of compounds in our body.

↩

....

8 So far as kids are concerned, they only like to play.

↩

....

9 Some people rely on government support to survive.

↩

....

10 Compressed air is very useful.

↩

....

11 A balloon can fly to the air because it is full of gas.

↩

....

12 Our environment is getting worse and worse.

↩

....

13 Vapor is critical to the formation of cloud.

↩

....

CHEMISTRY

13 *Periodic Table*

Students now all know the **periodic table**. This table was **invented** by the Russian scientist Dmitri Mendeleev. In the past, scientists discovered many elements and they also wished to have a table to **explain** these elements. Most people use the **properties** of the elements to **arrange** these elements. Mendeleev used **atomic number** to arrange the elements and he carefully examined again the atomic weights of many elements by doing a lot of **research**. In 1869, he published a periodic table with many **blanks** to show there were new elements to be discovered. He wrote a book entitled *The Principles of Chemistry* which explains many of his ideas. Dmitri Mendeleev passed away on 1907, aged 73.

　　現在的學生都知道元素週期表。這張表是俄國化學家迪米崔・門得列夫所發明的。在過去，科學家們發現了很多元素，他們當然也都希望有一張圖表可以解釋這些元素。大多數人都用元素的性質來排列這些元素。門得列夫是用元素的原子序來排列的，他做了很多研究，重新測量了很多元素的原子量。他在1869年列成了一張元素週期表，這張表格中有幾個空格，顯示這些元素當時還未被發現。他曾經寫過一本著作，叫做《化學原理》，這本書詳細地解釋了他的想法。迪米崔・門得列夫於1907年過世，享年73歲。

Vocabulary

periodic table 週期表	property (n.) 性質	research (n.) 研究
invent (v.) 發明	arrange (v.) 排列	blank (n.) 空格
explain (v.) 解釋	atomic number 原子序	

◇ The **periodic table** we use at present is very useful for us.
我們現在用的週期表對我們是很有用的。

◇ Edison **invented** many useful things. 愛迪生發明了很多有用的東西。

◇ How can you **explain** this peculiar experimental result?
你能如何解釋這項古怪的實驗結果？

◇ Each element has its unique **property**. 每一個元素都有獨特的性質。

◇ Elements are **arranged** in the present periodic table according to their atomic
numbers. 在目前的元素週期表，元素是根據原子序排列的。

◇ It is important for high school students to understand the meaning of **atomic
number**. 中學生瞭解原子序是很重要的。

◇ Scholars must do a lot of **research**. 學者必須做很多的研究。

◇ There are a lot of **blanks** in the table which you submitted.
你交來的表格裡有很多空格。

Translate the following sentences into Chinese

1 The periodic table we use at present tells us a lot about science.

....

2 Not everything invented by scientists is good for us.

....

3 You should work hard to be able to explain the experimental result.

....

4 Scientists make good use of the unique properties of chemical compounds.

....

5 The arrangement of elements in the present periodic table is really marvelous.

....

6 It is really amazing that every atomic number corresponds to a positive
integer and not a single positive integer is missing in the periodic table.

....

7 Scientists should avoid doing research which is harmful to human beings.

....

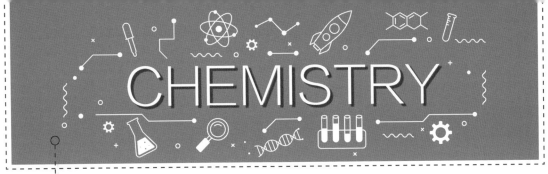

CHEMISTRY

14 *Madame Curie*

Madame Curie and her husband discovered **radium** and **plutonium**. They also discovered that radium can be used to **treat tumor**. Another **contribution** of Madame Curie was the theory of **radioactivity**. She invented **mobile** X-ray machines. This **allowed surgeons** to be able to treat injured soldiers. Madame Curie received Nobel Prizes in physics and chemistry. She was the first female who received Nobel Prize and the first person who received Nobel Prizes in two different **fields**.

居禮夫人和她的丈夫發現了鐳和釙,他們也發現了鐳元素可以被用來治療腫瘤。居禮夫人的另一貢獻是在放射性理論,她發明了移動式X光機,使得外科醫生可以治療傷兵。居禮夫人曾經得過諾貝爾物理和化學獎。她是第一位女性的諾貝爾獎得獎人,而且是歷史上唯一得到兩種不同科學領域諾貝爾獎的得主。

Vocabulary

radium (n.) 鐳

plutonium (n.) 釙

treat (v.) 治療

tumor (n.) 腫瘤

contribution (n.) 貢獻

radioactivity (n.) 放射性

mobile (a.) 可動的;移動式的

allow (v.) 使……可以;容許

surgeon (n.) 外科醫生

field (n.) 領域

Sentences

◇ **Radium** is radioactive. Every laboratory has to be very careful about it.
鐳有放射性，每個實驗室都要非常小心。

◇ **Plutonium** has something to do with the first atomic bomb. 鈽與第一個原子彈有關。

◇ Cancer patients are often **treated** with radiation. 放射性常用來治療癌症病人。

◇ Not every **tumor** is harmful. 並非所有腫瘤都是有害的。

◇ He had no **contribution** to human beings. 他對人類一無貢獻。

◇ **Radioactive** material is dangerous. 放射性物質是很危險的。

◇ Everyone uses **mobile** phone now. 現在人人都用手機了。

◇ X-ray machines **allow** doctors to examine patients effectively.
X 光機使得醫生可以有效地檢查病人。

◇ **Surgeons** cannot be too old. 外科醫生不能太老。

◇ He is not in the **field** of quantum mechanics. 他不在量子力學的領域。

Translate the following sentences into Chinese

1 Madame Curie and her husband worked very hard to extract radium.

2 Although radiation is useful in medical science, one still has to be careful about it.

3 One should go to a doctor if tumor is detected.

4 He had great contribution to human beings.

5 Radioactive material must be kept in a safe place.

6 Mobile phones are quite popular these days.

7 It is not easy to understand how X-ray machines work.

8 The salary of a surgeon is usually high.

9 One should always select a good field to get into.

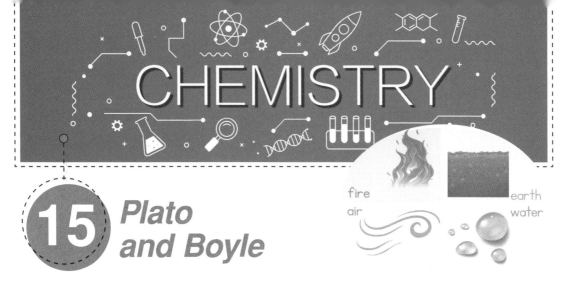

CHEMISTRY

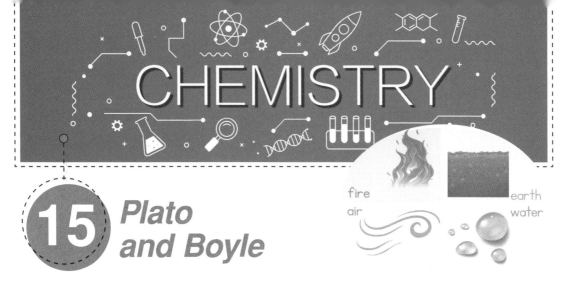

fire
air

earth
water

15 Plato and Boyle

About the **origin** of the **concept** of elements, the earliest person who had this idea was **Greek philosopher** Plato (300 BC). He thought that everything was **constructed** from some **basic** things. These things cannot be further **decomposed**. Plato called them elements and they were earth, water, fire and wind. Many **ancient** countries, such as **Egypt**, **Babylonia**, **Persia**, Japan and China also had similar concepts. In 1661, the Irish Chemist Boyle **criticized** the four elements theory. He **pointed out** that we cannot use these substances to create other substances, neither can we produce them from other substances. Boyle could be **considered** as the first person who **defined** elements from chemical **point of view**.

　　關於元素此一概念的由來，最早只是古希臘哲學家柏拉圖（西元前300年）提出的一個說法，他認為一切物質都是由最基本的物質所構成，而且這種物質不能再被分解為其他的東西。這個最基本的物質，柏拉圖就把它稱為元素，那就是「地、水、火、風的四元素說」。很多古國，如埃及、巴比倫尼亞、波斯、日本和中國都有類似的觀念。1661年，愛爾蘭化學家波以耳批判了一直存在的四元素說，他指出我們無法用這四個元素來製造別的物質，也無法從別的物質中取得這些元素。波以耳被認為是歷史上第一位從化學的觀點來定義元素的人。

Vocabulary

origin (n.) 由來；起源
concept (n.) 觀念；概念
Greek (a.) 希臘的 /
(n.) 希臘人
philosopher (n.) 哲學家
construct (v.) 構成

basic (a.) 基本的
decompose (v.) 分解
ancient (a.) 古代的
Egypt (n.) 埃及
Babylonia
(n.) 巴比倫尼亞

Persia (n.) 波斯
criticize (v.) 批判
point out 指出
consider (v.) 認為
define (v.) 定義
point of view 觀點

◇ We should investigate the **origin** of the virus. 我們應該調查此病毒從何而來。

◇ His **concept** of radiation was wrong. 他對放射性的觀念是錯的。

◇ There were a lot of **Greek philosophers**. 希臘有很多哲學家。

◇ It is hard to understand **philosophy**. 哲學是很難懂的。

◇ We have to understand the **construction** of an atom.
我們應該瞭解原子是如何構成的。

◇ This knowledge is very **basic**. 這個學問是很基本的。

◇ Chemists are able to **decompose** material. 化學家能分解物質。

◇ In **ancient** days, people did not understand the nature as we do now.
在過去，古代人對大自然的瞭解比不上我們。

◇ **Egypt** has a very long history. 埃及有很長的歷史。

◇ **Babylonia** was an ancient country. 巴比倫尼亞是一個古老的國家。

◇ **Persia** is now called Iran. 波斯現在叫做伊朗。

◇ He **criticized** the use of atomic bombs. 他批判使用原子彈。

◇ He **pointed out** the weakness of the theory. 他指出這個理論的弱點。

◇ I **considered** that he is totally wrong. 我認為他全錯了。

◇ Two points **define** a line. 兩點決定一條直線。

◇ His **point of view** is marvelous. 他的觀點實在精彩。

 Translate the following sentences into Chinese

1 The origin of the virus is still unknown.

☞
....

2 No one understands his concept.

☞
....

3 Greek philosophers had great influence on civilization.

☞
....

4 Philosophy is often too vague for us.

ᶜ⊛

....

5 Do you know how this theory is constructed?

ᶜ⊛

....

6 Although this knowledge is basic, it is still important.

ᶜ⊛

....

7 Elements cannot be further decomposed.

ᶜ⊛

....

8 We actually do not know how ancient people lived.

ᶜ⊛

....

9 Ancient Egyptian scientists had great contribution to science and mathematics. ᶜ⊛

....

10 The country of Babylonia no longer exists.

ᶜ⊛

....

11 Persia was a powerful country before.

ᶜ⊛

....

12 Hitler is widely criticized.

ᶜ⊛

....

13 He pointed out the danger of climate change.

ᶜ⊛

....

14 I consider that he is a clever student.

ᶜ⊛

....

15 Many present scientific terms are defined by using advanced theories.

ᶜ⊛

....

16 He took the action from the point of view of helping the poor.

ᶜ⊛

....

CHEMISTRY

16 *Lavoisier and Element*

In 1774, the British chemist Priestly found a gas which helped things burn. This gas was named "oxygen" by the French **aristocrat** chemist Antoine Lavoisier (At that time, people were not **certain** whether oxygen was an element.) and in 1777, he **suggested** that the burning of a material was a result of the chemical reaction of oxygen and the material. Lavoisier **conducted** a **series** of chemical experiments based upon the idea of Boyle. He finally **determined** many matters to be elements because he could not **design** any experiment to decompose these matters. Lavoisier also considered light and heat as elements, **indicating** that he was still **influenced** by the ancient Greek philosophers.

　　1774年，英國化學家卜利士力發現一種有助燃作用的氣體，被法國貴族的化學家拉瓦節命名為「氧」（這時候還不能確定氧是元素），並在1777年提出物質燃燒是氧與物質反應的結果。拉瓦節根據波以耳對元素的定義，進行了一連串的化學實驗，最後決定了很多物質是元素，因為他無法設計任何實驗來分解這些物質。拉瓦節當時也認定光和熱是元素，顯示他仍受古時希臘哲學家的影響。

Vocabulary

aristocrat (n.) 貴族	determine (v.) 決定
certain (a.) 確定的	design (n.) (v.) 設計
suggest (v.) 提出	indicate (v.) 顯示；指出
conduct (v.) 進行	influence (v.) 影響
series (n.) 連串；系列	

Sentences

◇ There are still many **aristocrats** in this world. 世界上仍有很多貴族。

◇ We cannot be **certain** about many things of Nature.
我們對大自然的很多事情都無法確定的。

◇ In the ancient days, people **suggested** the idea that the sun goes around the earth.
古時候，人們提出太陽繞地球轉的想法。

◇ A lot of experiments were **conducted** by Faraday. 法拉第進行過很多實驗。

◇ A **series** of explosions occurred last night. 昨晚發生了一連串的爆炸。

◇ He cannot **determine** whether he should do this research.
他無法決定是否該做這個研究。

◇ He **designed** this famous experiment. 他設計了這個有名的實驗。

◇ This **indicates** that he is quite clear-minded. 這顯示他仍然思路清晰。

◇ He was strongly **influenced** by his father. 他受他父親影響很深。

Translate the following sentences into Chinese

1 He suggested repeating the experiment again.

2 We cannot be certain whether it will rain tomorrow.

3 Actually, the present aristocrats do not have much privilege.

4 These experiments were not conducted correctly.

5 He made a series of mistakes.

6 He determined that the experimental result was not correct.

7 He designed this bridge.

8 This indicated that a big storm will hit us.

9 His friends had bad influences on him.

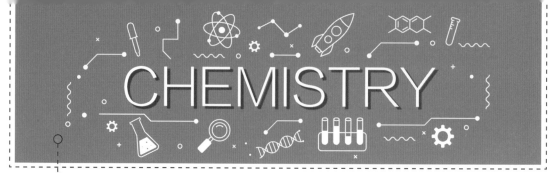

CHEMISTRY

17 Air

Air is **touched** by every human being, but it has no color, no **smell** and no taste. Therefore we cannot see the air. Scientists discovered that water exists in air. In the dry air, the largest amount of gas is **nitrogen**. The oxygen **follows**. Of course, there are small amount of carbon dioxide and **ozone** in the air. Nitrogen is very **stable** and will hardly **react** with other substances, but it is very useful in industries. Oxygen is something that human beings **rely on** to live. Without oxygen, there will be no living organisms.

　空氣是人類一定會接觸到的，可是因為它無色、無臭、無味，所以我們看不見空氣。科學家發現空氣中有水氣。乾燥的空氣中最多的是氮氣，第二多的是氧氣，當然還有微量的二氧化碳和臭氧等等。氮氣非常穩定，幾乎不會和其他物質起化學反應，但在工業上有很多功用。氧氣是人類賴以生存的氣體。如果沒有氧氣，生物不可能生存。

Vocabulary

touch (v.) 接觸；碰觸

smell (n.) 氣味

nitrogen (n.) 氮氣

follow (v.) 跟隨

ozone (n.) 臭氧

stable (a.) 穩定的

react (v.) 反應

rely on　依賴

Sentences

◇ When we **touch** air, we cannot feel its existence.
我們碰到空氣的時候，無法感受到它的存在。

◇ Sometimes, we require a chemical compound to absolutely have no **smell**.
我們有時會要求一個化學品必須絕對沒有氣味。

◇ **Nitrogen** was discovered by three British scientists as an element in 1772.
三位英國科學家在 1772 年發現氮氣是元素。

◇ Do not blindly **follow** others. 不要盲從。

◇ **Ozone** exists high above the earth. 臭氧存在於離地球很高的地方。

◇ A good machine must be **stable**. 好的機器必須是穩定的。

◇ He has no **reaction** to my request. 他對我的要求毫無反應。

◇ This company totally **relies on** technology of foreign countries.
這家公司完全依賴外國的技術。

 Translate the following sentences into Chinese

1 Don't touch this research topic. It is a very difficult one.

2 It is hard to detect whether a compound has smell or not.

3 Ammonia contains nitrogen.

4 Ozone layer in the atmosphere prevents some damaging light from reaching the earth.

5 The following figure contains an amplifier circuit.

6 Not all elements are stable.

7 His reaction to the news is sadness.

8 We cannot totally rely on the subsidy from the government.

CHEMISTRY

18 Carbon Dioxide and Carbon Monoxide

Carbon dioxide is one of the gases in the air. After we human beings breathe, we release carbon dioxide. If there are plants nearby, they will absorb it to execute photosynthesis. If the burning of any substance containing carbon is not complete, carbon monoxide will be produced. If one person intakes too much carbon monoxide, he will be in the state of lacking oxygen which is dangerous. If the burning of natural gas used in households is not complete, carbon monoxide will also be made. If too much carbon dioxide is released, sunlight cannot be reflected back. This will cause the temperature of earth's surface to go up.

二氧化碳是空氣中的一種氣體。人呼吸以後會釋放二氧化碳。如果附近有植物,植物會吸收二氧化碳來進行光合作用。若含碳物質在燃燒過程中燃燒不完全則會產生一氧化碳。人體如果吸入過量的一氧化碳就會發生缺氧現象,非常危險。家庭使用的天然氣如果燃燒不完全,也會產生一氧化碳。二氧化碳如果排放過多,會使得太陽光無法反射回去,因此會使地球表面溫度增加。

Vocabulary

breathe (v.) 呼吸／
breath (n.) 呼吸

release (v.) 釋放

absorb (v.) 吸收

execute (v.) 進行;執行

synthesis (n.) 合成／ synthesize (v.) 合成

carbon monoxide 一氧化碳

Sentences

◇ A man will be in serious situation if his **breathing** stops for even a very short time.
人如呼吸停止一小段時間，都是很危險的。

◇ The **releasing** of a large amount of carbon dioxide is harmful.
大量二氧化碳的釋放是有害的。

◇ Luckily, plants **absorb** carbon dioxide. 幸運的是，植物會吸收二氧化碳。

◇ Nature **executes** many amazing chemical processes.
大自然進行很多奇異的化學作用。

◇ DNA cannot be **synthesized** by us. 我們無法合成 DNA。

◇ **Carbon monoxide** is toxic. 一氧化碳是有毒的。

 Translate the following sentences into Chinese

1 In a hospital, oxygen is needed to help patients to breathe.

　☞ ....

2 We must be sure that poisonous gas will not be released from factories.

　☞ ....

3 It is hard for old people to absorb new knowledge.

　☞ ....

4 Many chemical processes are executed in our body all the time.

　☞ ....

5 Synthesized fur can still keep us warm.

　☞ ....

6 We should never let our kitchen be sealed because carbon monoxide may be accumulated this way.

　☞ ....

19 *Global Warming*

We often use **greenhouse** to grow flowers. Greenhouses are usually made out of glass so that sunlight can easily get into it. However, it is hard for sunlight to leave the greenhouse. Therefore, the temperature inside the greenhouse is kept quite high. If the amount of carbon dioxide and **methane** increases, it will **prevent** sunlight from **reflecting** back. Therefore the **phenomenon** of **global warming** occurs. The increasing of carbon dioxide started from the **industrial revolution** with the burning of coal, **petroleum** and natural gas. The global warming makes the ice of the north and south melt and leads to the rising of **sea-level**.

　　種花常常使用溫室。溫室多半全是玻璃做的，所以陽光可以進入溫室。然而陽光不容易離開溫室。因此，溫室內的溫度可以保持地相當高。二氧化碳及甲烷如果增加，也會防止太陽光反射回去，因此地球暖化的現象就發生了。二氧化碳的增加起始自人類的工業革命，是燃燒煤炭、石油與天然氣等等的結果。地球暖化的結果，導致北極和南極的冰層融化，以及海平面上升。

Vocabulary

greenhouse　溫室
methane (n.) 甲烷
prevent (v.) 防止
reflect (v.) 反射
phenomenon (n.) 現象

global warming
地球暖化
revolution　革命
industrial revolution
工業革命

petroleum (n.) 石油
sea-level　海平面

Sentences

◇ The **greenhouse** effect causes global warming. 溫室效應造成全球暖化。

◇ **Methane** exists under the surface of the earth. 甲烷藏在地球表面之下。

◇ We must be able to **prevent** natural disasters from inflicting heavy damages on us. 我們一定要防止自然災害對我們造成重大損失。

◇ Mirrors **reflect** light. 鏡子反射光。

◇ This strange **phenomenon** should be thoroughly investigated. 這個奇怪的現象應被澈底調查。

◇ **Global warming** is a serious matter. 地球暖化是一件嚴重的事情。

◇ Modern technology **revolutionized** our civilization. 現代科技對我們的文明有革命性的影響。

◇ **Industrial revolution** is beneficial to us, but it also has bad effects. 工業革命對我們是好的，但也有壞處。

◇ The use of **petroleum** causes air pollution. 使用石油會造成空氣污染。

◇ The **sea-level** has been rising. 海平面一直在上升。

Translate the following sentences into Chinese

1 It is expensive to keep a greenhouse. ☞

2 Methane is an important part of the natural gas.
☞

3 Many natural disasters cannot be prevented.
☞

4 Microscope uses the fact that light can be reflected.
☞

5 It is hard to explain this peculiar phenomenon.
☞

6 Global warming will harm many countries.
☞

7 This technology is quite revolutionary. ☞

8 Industrial revolution was a significant event in the history.
☞

9 Petroleum is important to our living standard.
☞

10 The rising of sea-level will make many islands disappear.
☞

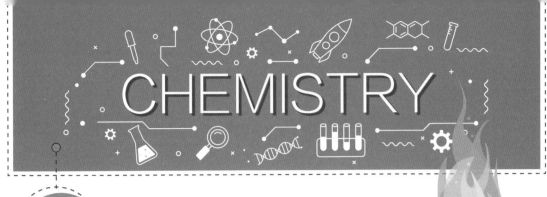

CHEMISTRY

20 Oxidation and Reduction

Burning is a result of the combination of oxygen and some material. The **rusting** of metal is also related to oxygen. Therefore, scientists name the reaction between oxygen and material to be **oxidization**. Some material cannot be easily oxidized, but some can. Gold can be kept in the air for a long time without being oxidized, but sodium is easy to be oxidized. If a material loses oxygen, the reaction is called **reduction**. In Nature, there are many metals which can be easily oxidized. Therefore, they often exist in the world in the form of compounds. To **extract pure** metal, we must use reduction. The **breathing** of **living organisms** is an oxidization and photosynthesis is reduction. Both oxidization and reduction are important to Nature.

　　燃燒是氧與物質結合的結果。金屬生鏽也與氧有關。因此，科學家將物質與氧的化學反應稱為氧化反應。有些物質不容易被氧化，也有些物質很容易被氧化。黃金可以在空氣中保存很久而不被氧化，但是鈉就極容易被氧化。如果物質失去氧，這種反應叫做還原反應。自然界很多金屬是很容易被氧化的，所以在自然界中，它們是以化合物的形式存在的。要提煉出純金屬，必須要用還原的原理。我們可以說，生物的呼吸是氧化反應，而光合作用乃是還原反應。氧化和還原對自然界都是相當重要的。

 Vocabulary

rust (v.) 生鏽
oxidization (n.) 氧化
reduction (n.) 【化】還原
extract (v.) 提煉

pure (a.) 純的
breathe (v.) 呼吸
living organism　生物

Sentences

◇ Only metals can **rust**.
只有金屬會生鏽。

◇ **Oxidization** happens everywhere in the world.
氧化在世界各地發生。

◇ The chemical process to remove rust from rusted metals is a **reduction** process.
去掉金屬的鏽是一種還原作用。

◇ In the ancient days, people worked hard to **extract** precious metals, such as gold from compounds. 古時候，人們喜歡從化合物中提煉貴重金屬，例如金子。

◇ It is hard to obtain a **pure** compound. 純化合物是很難取得的。

◇ One dies when his **breathing** stops. 呼吸停止，人就死了。

◇ Plants and animals are **living organisms**. 動植物都是生物。

Translate the following sentences into Chinese

1 Silver tableware can rust. ✍

....

2 Oxidization may be harmful to our health.

✍

....

3 The chemical reduction process is a process of gaining electrons.

✍

....

4 The method to extract precious metals is called alchemy.

✍

....

5 His theory is purely based upon mathematics.

✍

....

6 Breathing needs oxygen.

✍

....

7 It is hard to totally understand living organisms.

✍

....

PART 3

PHYSICS

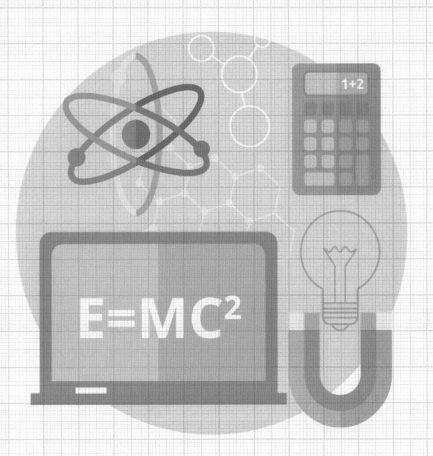

PHYSICS

01 Time

Long time ago, when there was no **written language** to **express** the past, present and future, we **discovered** the **concept** of time. However, if each of us has different ideas about time, there will be **difficulties** in **communicating** among people. For example, my friend and I are going out to play at about 9 o'clock in the morning. But people in ancient times did not have watches, nor did they have clocks at home. Maybe it was 9:30 when I got up, but the poor friend was waiting for me at 7:50 in the morning. Therefore, **in order to facilitate communication**, smart humans began to find ways to **define** time, and **reached** a **consensus** about time.

古時候，在有文字之前，人類為了表示過去、現在和未來，我們發現了時間的概念。但是如果我們每個人對於時間的觀念並不相同，那人們之間要溝通就會有困難。例如我和朋友要出去玩，約在早上9點鐘，可是古時候的人並沒有手錶，家裡也沒有時鐘。可能我起床的時候已經9點30分了，那位可憐的朋友卻在早上7點50分就在那邊等我了。所以說，為了要方便溝通，聰明的人們就開始找尋定義時間的方法，並達成對時間的共識。

Vocabulary

written language 文字
express (v.) 表示；表達
discover (v.) 發現
concept (n.) 概念；觀念
difficulty (n.) 困難
communicate (v.) 溝通

in order to 為了
facilitate (v.) 使方便、便利；促進
communication (n.) 溝通
define (v.) 定義
reach (v.) 達成
consensus (n.) 共識

Sentences

◇ Not every human race has **written language**. 並非每個民族都有文字。

◇ He has already **expressed** his opinion rather clearly. 他已將他的意見表示得很清楚。

◇ A new star was **discovered** lately by some scientists in Africa.
一些非洲的科學家最近發現了一顆新星。

◇ This is an old **concept**. 這是一個古老的觀念。

◇ We have to overcome this **difficulty**. 我們一定要克服這個困難。

◇ It is hard to **communicate** with old people. 和老人溝通是很困難的。

◇ **In order to** be a good scientist, we must be good in mathematics.
要當一個好的科學家，要先學好數學。

◇ To **facilitate** people's commute to work, the city provides a convenient
bus system. 為了使人們便於上班工作，市政府提供了便利的公共汽車系統。

◇ **Communication** is very important to the security of a nation.
通訊對國家安全是很重要的。

◇ Two points **define** a line. 兩點決定一條直線。

◇ We still cannot **reach** an agreement. 我們尚未能達成協議。

◇ There is no **consensus** about how to solve this problem.
對於如何解決此問題，仍無共識。

Translate the following sentences into Chinese

1 Only a few human races have written languages.

⌒⊸

....

2 He cannot express his idea clearly.

⌒⊸

....

3 An old tomb was discovered lately in Africa.

⌒⊸

....

4 This new concept is well accepted by all of us.

⌒⊸

....

5 It is by no means easy to overcome this difficulty.

✎

....

6 We have to be careful when we communicate with patients.

✎

....

7 In order to be an athlete, we must be strong.

✎

....

8 To facilitate students' study, the city opens all libraries.

✎

....

9 The 5G communication system is quite expensive.

✎

....

10 Three points define a plane.

✎

....

11 It is hard to reach our original goal.

✎

....

12 That we should have a good economy is a consensus of our society.

✎

....

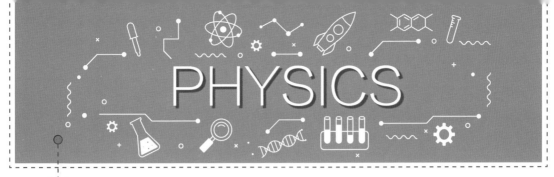

PHYSICS

02 The Significance of Time to Ancient People

In **ancient** times, humans did not define time in order to **hang out** with friends. It was to understand the changes of the four **seasons**. Why should we understand the changes of the four seasons? This is because when humans made **progress** from the hunting age to the farming age, it was important to know what **crops** to grow in what season. If you **miss** the time for **planting**, the **consequences** will be **serious**, and there may be **famine** in the whole country.

在古老的年代，人們定義時間當然不是因為要和朋友出去玩，而是為了要了解四季的變化。為什麼要了解四季的變化呢？這是因為當人類從狩獵時代進步到農耕時代，知道在什麼季節種什麼作物是很重要的。如果錯過了耕種的時機，那後果可是會很嚴重的，可能整個國家都會鬧飢荒。

Vocabulary

ancient (a.) 古老的

hang out 玩耍；閒晃

season (n.) 季節

progress (n.) 進步

crop (n.) 作物

miss (v.) 錯過

plant (v.) 播種

consequence (n.) 後果

serious (a.) 嚴重的

famine (n.) 飢荒

◇ This is an **ancient** machine which is not used anymore.
這是一個古老的機器，已經沒有人用了。

◇ This is a place where young people like to **hang out**.
這是一個年輕人喜歡去玩耍的地方。

◇ This is not a **season** for swimming. 這不是適合游泳的季節。

◇ He has not made any **progress** in his research. 他在研究上毫無進展。

◇ Farmers know when to harvest **crops**. 農人知道何時收成農作物。

◇ Do not **miss** the good opportunity. 不要錯過這個好機會。

◇ These crops are **planted** in spring. 這些農作物在春天撥種。

◇ The **consequence** of a wrong decision is always serious.
錯誤決定的後果永遠是很嚴重的。

◇ This is a **serious** problem. 這是一個嚴重的問題。

◇ The war will cause a **famine** in our country. 戰爭會帶給我國飢荒。

Translate the following sentences into Chinese

1 This is an ancient vase which is very valuable. ✑

2 Summer is a typhoon season. ✑

3 He has made good progress in promoting his work.
✑

4 A storm may destroy crops. ✑

5 Do not miss the train. ✑

6 Beautiful flowers are planted in this garden. ✑

7 You must know the possible consequence before you make a decision.
✑

8 His condition is getting more and more serious.
✑

9 Famine occurs frequently in this poor country.
✑

PHYSICS

03 Calendars

In all ancient **civilizations**, as long as they had **developed agriculture**, their **calendars** were very **sophisticated**. For example, to name a few: the ancient **Mayan** calendar in South America, the ancient **Egyptian** calendar in the middle east which was called the **Coptic** calendar, the ancient **Persian** calendar in the middle east, called the **Iranian** calendar, and the Chinese calendar in Asia, called the **Peasant** Calendar. These calendars have their own way of calculating time, and they are very **accurate**. Yet to reach these **achievements**, we need not only **well-developed** mathematical ability, but also very **advanced astronomical observation** ability. It can be seen that these ancient people were very smart!

在所有的古文明中，只要是農業發達的文明，他們的曆法（計算時間的方法）都很先進。像在南美洲古馬雅的曆法——馬雅曆、在中東古埃及的曆法——科普特曆、中東古波斯的曆法——伊朗曆，還有在亞洲中國的曆法——農民曆，這些曆法都有他們自己計算時間的方式，也非常地準確。但要達到這些成就，除了必須具備高度發展的數學能力，還要有非常進步的天文觀測能力，可見這些古代人都是非常聰明的呢！

Vocabulary

civilization (n.) 文明
develop (v.) 發展
agriculture (n.) 農業
calendar (n.) 曆法
sophisticated (a.)
先進的；複雜的
Mayan (a.) 馬雅族的

Egyptian (a.) 埃及的
Coptic (a.)
（古埃及）科普特的
Persian (a.) 波斯的
Iranian (a.) 伊朗的
peasant (n.) 農民
accurate (a.) 準確的

achievement (n.) 成就
well-developed (a.)
高度發展的
advanced (a.) 進步的
astronomical (a.) 天文的
observation (n.) 觀測

Sentences

◇ Ancient **civilizations** are interesting. 古文明是很有趣的。

◇ The industry of our country is well **developed**. 我們國家的工業很發達。

◇ **Agriculture** is important for every country. 對任何國家而言，農業都是重要的。

◇ The most popular calendar in the world is the Gregorian **Calendar**.
世界上最多人用的曆法是格雷葛曆法。

◇ This is a **sophisticated** instrument. 這是一個先進的設備。

◇ The **Mayan** civilization has disappeared. 馬雅文明已經消失了。

◇ There are many pyramids in **Egypt**. 埃及有很多金字塔。

◇ The **Coptic** Church is a Christian church. 科普特教會是基督教派。

◇ **Iranians** are **Persians**. 伊朗人是波斯人。

◇ We should pay attention to the welfare of **peasants** of our country.
我們應該注意我國農民的福利。

◇ I have an **accurate** clock. 我有一個準確的時鐘。

◇ He has tremendous **achievements.** 他的成就非凡。

◇ Japan is a **well-developed** country. 日本是一個發展良好的國家。

◇ It is important to have **advanced** technologies. 有進步的技術是很重要的。

◇ **Astronomical** observation helped many scientists, including Newton.
天文觀察幫助了很多科學家，包含牛頓在內。

◇ Did you **observe** how the students react to your lecturing?
你有沒有觀察學生對你教學的反應？

Translate the following sentences into Chinese

1 Different civilizations create different countries.

   ↺

2 This branch of science has been well developed.

   ↺

3 Agriculture is a branch of science now.

   ↺

4   The Muslim countries have their own calendars.

    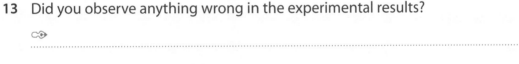
    ....

5   This machine is not sophisticated.

    ☞
    ....

6   Sine and cosine were invented in Egypt.

    ☞
    ....

7   The Coptic Church still exists in Egypt.

    ☞
    ....

8   We should always respect peasants.

    ☞
    ....

9   This instrument measures distance accurately.

    ☞
    ....

10 He has no achievement at all.

    ☞
    ....

11 Unfortunately, we don't have many advanced technologies.

    ☞
    ....

12 Sophisticated astronomical observation is very expensive these days.

    ☞
    ....

13 Did you observe anything wrong in the experimental results?

    ☞
    ....

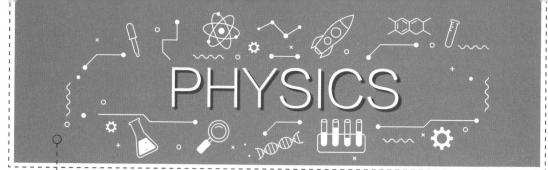

PHYSICS

04 *Galileo–I*

In 1583, the Italian scientist Galileo Galilei was still an 18-year-old medical student. One day he was in the church and found that the **chandelier** was **shaking**. Out of **curiosity**, Galileo used his **pulses** to **measure** the period of the chandelier **swings** (the so-called period is the time it takes to swing back and forth once). He unexpectedly discovered that although the **amplitude** of the swing of the chandelier is getting smaller and smaller, the period is a **constant**. This is how Galileo discovered the "**isochronism** of a simple **pendulum**."

在1583年時，正當義大利科學家伽利略‧伽利萊還是一個18歲的醫學院學生時，某天他在教堂裡，發現吊燈在晃動。出於好奇心，伽利略以脈搏測量吊燈擺動的週期（所謂週期就是來回擺動一次所需的時間）。他不經意地發現：吊燈擺動的幅度雖然愈來愈小，但週期卻是固定的，伽利略就是由此發現「單擺的等時性」。

Vocabulary

chandelier (n.) 吊燈

shake (v.) 晃動

curiosity (n.) 好奇心

pulse (n.) 脈搏；脈衝

measure (v.) 測量

swing (n.) (v.) 擺動

amplitude (n.) 幅度

constant (n.) 不變的事物

isochronism (n.) 等時性

pendulum (n.) 單擺

 Sentences

◇ **Chandeliers** are widely used in cathedrals. 大教堂裡常使用吊燈。

◇ A good machine does not **shake**. 好的機械不會晃動。

◇ A good scientist is always full of **curiosity**. 好的科學家一定永遠有好奇心。

◇ Digital circuits use **pulses** to represent data. 數位線路使用脈衝來表示資料。

◇ It is difficult to **measure** a very small signal. 測量小訊號是很難的。

◇ Those bells **swing** every Sunday morning. 那些鐘每個星期日早上都會擺動。

◇ The **amplitude** of the output signal cannot be too small. 輸出訊號幅度不能太小。

◇ The output of a power supply circuit must be a **constant**.
電源供應器的輸出必須是固定的。

◇ **Pendulums** are used in grandfather clocks. 大型座鐘內都用了單擺。

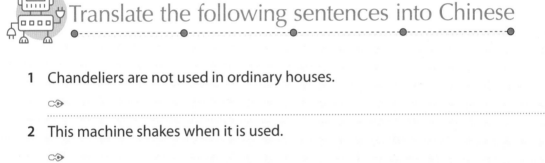 Translate the following sentences into Chinese

1 Chandeliers are not used in ordinary houses.

2 This machine shakes when it is used.

3 If you do not have any curiosity, you will never become a good scientist.

4 It is not easy to create good pulses in a digital circuit.

5 It is difficult to measure a very short distance precisely.

6 The top of trees swings.

7 An amplifier magnifies the amplitude of a signal.

8 The temperature inside a precision machine must be kept a constant.

PHYSICS

05 Galileo-II

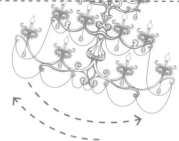

He further studied the nature of the pendulum by experiments and found that the period of a single pendulum swinging is only **related** to the length of the pendulum. When the length of the pendulum is shorter, the period of the single pendulum is smaller. That is, it can swing more times in the same duration of time and the mass of the pendulum will not **affect** the **cycle** of the pendulum." Galileo's discovery was a **pioneering work**, although he was younger than twenty years old. But from this we can see that his **potential** was **limitless**. **No wonder** he could become a **pioneer** in the development of **modern** physics in the future.

　他再進一步實驗研究單擺的性質後發現：「單擺的週期僅與擺長有關。當單擺的擺長愈短，單擺的週期愈小。即在相同時間內，可擺動次數愈多，而擺錘的質量不會影響單擺的週期。」伽利略的發現在當時是個創舉，雖然當年他還未滿20歲，但從此就可看出他的潛力無可限量，難怪能在日後成為現代物理學發展的先驅。

Vocabulary

related (a.) 有關的

affect (v.) 影響

cycle (n.) 週期

pioneering work 創舉

potential (n.) 潛力

limitless (a.) 無限的

no wonder 難怪

pioneer (n.) 先驅

modern (a.) 現代的

 Sentences

◇ This problem is not **related** to chemistry. 這問題和化學無關。

◇ Temperature will **affect** the result of an experiment. 溫度會影響實驗的結果。

◇ If the **cycle** of an oscillation is short, its frequency is high.
如果震動的週期短，它的頻率就會高。

◇ His research is really a **pioneering work**. 他的研究真是創舉。

◇ He has great **potential** to be a brilliant scientist. 他有潛力成為一個傑出的科學家。

◇ He works very hard. **No wonder** he succeeds. 他努力工作，難怪他成功了。

◇ He is a **pioneer** in abstract mathematics. 他是抽象數學的先驅。

◇ He started the study of **modern** physics. 他開啟了現代物理的研究。

 Translate the following sentences into Chinese

1 This problem is closely related to physics.

   ↪ ....

2 Both temperature and pressure will affect the function of the machine.

   ↪ ....

3 The frequency of an oscillation is reversely related to its cycle.

   ↪ ....

4 His research is actually not a pioneering work. A lot of people did this kind of
   research years ago. ↪

   ....

5 Every student has some kind of potential.

   ↪ ....

6 He never exercises. No wonder he is not strong.

   ↪ ....

7 He is a pioneer in communication technology.

   ↪ ....

8 Modern physics is difficult. ↪

   ....

06 Length–I

About the **definition** of "**meter**," since the eighteenth **century**, there has been a long **course** of **evolution**. After the French **Revolution** in 1789, the French **established** a **committee** to **promote** the **metric system**. Their **resolution** was to take the earth as the **standard**, and define the length of the longitude line from the **North Pole** to the **equator** through Paris as 10 million meters. Dividing this **distance** by ten million, you can get the length of one meter as the standard length in meters. They finally made a **platinum-iridium alloy** called the "**international prototype** meter" as the standard length of a meter. However, since the measurement technology was not yet **mature** at that time, the "international prototype meter" produced based on the measurement results at that time had an error of 0.2 mm compared to the current length of 1 meter.

關於「米」（慣稱公尺）的定義，自十八世紀以來，有一段時間不算短的演化過程。1789年法國大革命後，法國人為了推廣公制，設立了一個委員會。決議以地球為標準，將北極到赤道通過巴黎的經線長定義為一千萬米，而這段距離除以一千萬，就可以得到一米的長度，作為米單位的標準長度。他們最後以此標準長度製作出了鉑銥合金的「國際公尺原器」。不過由於當時測量技術尚未成熟，當時依測量結果製作出的「國際公尺原器」與現今1米的長度相比，有0.2毫米的誤差。

Vocabulary

definition (n.) 定義
meter (n.) 米（慣稱公尺）
century (n.) 世紀
course (n.) 過程
evolution (n.) 演化
revolution (n.) 革命
establish (v.) 設立

committee (n.) 委員會
promote (v.) 推廣
metric system 公制
resolution (n.) 決議
standard (n.) 標準
North Pole 北極
equator (n.) 赤道

distance (n.) 距離
platinum (n.) 鉑
iridium (n.) 銥
alloy (n.) 合金
international (a.) 國際的
prototype (n.) 原型
mature (a.) 成熟的

Sentences

◇ Do you know the **definition** of voltage? 你知道伏特的定義嗎？

◇ Most countries use **meter** to measure distance. 多數國家用公尺來測量距離。

◇ A **century** consists of one hundred years. 一個世紀包含一百年。

◇ Many events happen in the **course** of a revolution. 很多事在革命的過程中發生。

◇ The theory of **evolution** explains many natural phenomena.
演化論解釋了很多自然界的現象。

◇ In a democratic country, **revolution** is not needed. 民主國家不需要革命。

◇ We should always obey the international **standard**. 我們必須遵守國際標準。

◇ We **established** a **committee** to solve the problem.
我們設立了一個委員會來解決這個問題。

◇ We should **promote** scientific research. 我們應該推廣科學研究。

◇ Only a few countries do not use the **metric system**. 只有少數國家不用公制。

◇ The **resolution** of the conference is to reject his proposal.
會議的決議拒絕了他的建議。

◇ It is always cold in the **North Pole**. 北極永遠很冷。

◇ It is always hot in the **equator**. 赤道總是很熱。

◇ Do you know how to measure **distance**? 你知道如何測量距離嗎？

◇ It is hard to make an **alloy**. 製造合金是很困難的。

◇ This is an **international** problem. 這是一個國際問題。

◇ We have produced a **prototype** of the machine. 我們已製造了這台機器的原型樣品。

◇ This technology is not **mature** yet. 這個技術尚未成熟。

# Translate the following sentences into Chinese

1 The definition of any term in mathematics is important.

2 This happened centuries ago.

3 People suffer in revolutions.

4 The theory of evolution does not explain every natural phenomenon.

5 We established a committee to study the problem.

6 We should promote the study of mathematics.

7 It is foolish not to use the metric system.

8 The resolution of the conference is to accept his proposal.

9 The ice of the North Pole is melting.

10 It is hard to measure distances precisely.

11 Large corporations define the international industrial standard.

12 The Equator divides the earth into two parts.

13 Many industrial parts are made of alloy.

14 We should pay attention to international news.

15 It is difficult to produce even a prototype of this machine.

16 This technology is quite mature now.

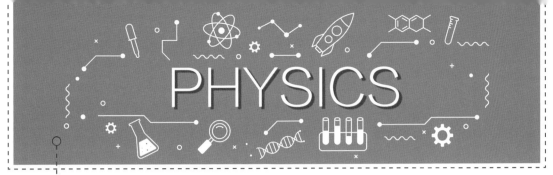

PHYSICS

07 Length–II

The students may have questions. Did the French really go to the North Pole? Of course not! Two French scientists spent seven years to **measure** the distance from Dunkirk in France to Barcelona in Spain. **Based upon** this result, they were able to **obtain** the **length** of 1 meter. As for how they measured it, it involved **astronomy**, **trigonometry**, **geometry**, etc. If students are interested in the stories, they can find the book *The Birth of the Meter* (by Ken Alder) to read.

同學們可能會產生疑問,那法國人真的到北極去了嗎?當然沒有!兩位法國科學家花了七年時間測量了從法國的敦克爾克到西班牙的巴塞隆納的距離。根據這個結果,他們就可以得到1米的長度。至於他們是如何測量的,則牽涉到天文學、三角學與幾何學等等。如果同學們對其中的故事有興趣的話,可以去找一本書叫做《公尺的誕生》(作者肯·阿爾德)來閱讀。

Vocabulary

measure (v.) 測量

based upon 根據

obtain (v.) 得到

length (n.) 長度

astronomy (n.) 天文學

trigonometry (n.) 三角學

geometry (n.) 幾何學

◇ Did you **measure** your weight? 你量體重了嗎？

◇ Your statements should always be **based upon** facts. 你的話都要根據事實。

◇ It is hard to **obtain** a diploma of master's degree. 得到碩士文憑是很難的。

◇ The **length** of my new car is shorter than that of my old car.
我新車的長度比舊車的長度短。

◇ The **astronomy** is a study of the universe. 天文學是研究宇宙的學問。

◇ **Trigonometry** involves sine and cosine. 三角學牽涉到了正弦和餘弦。

◇ **Geometry** involves logical thinking. 幾何學牽涉到邏輯思考。

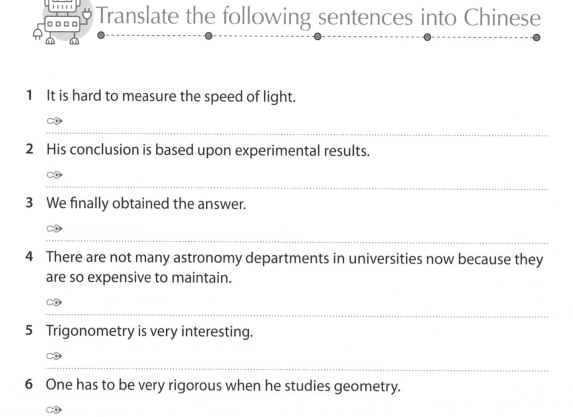 Translate the following sentences into Chinese

1 It is hard to measure the speed of light.

ↄ๏ ....

2 His conclusion is based upon experimental results.

ↄ๏ ....

3 We finally obtained the answer.

ↄ๏ ....

4 There are not many astronomy departments in universities now because they are so expensive to maintain.

ↄ๏ ....

5 Trigonometry is very interesting.

ↄ๏ ....

6 One has to be very rigorous when he studies geometry.

ↄ๏ ....

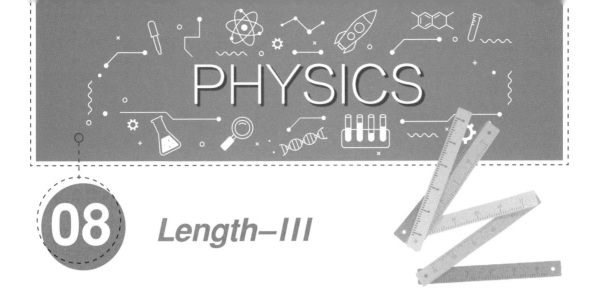

PHYSICS

08 Length–III

In 1875, many countries **signed** the "Metric **Convention**." They **jointly** developed the metric system and **coordinated** the **conversion** of different international systems of units, and **in order to** make the convention **operational**, the "**Bureau** international des poids et mesures (BIPM for brief)" was established in the **suburb** of Paris in the same year. From then on, the **global** metric system began to **unfold**. The Bureau international des poids et mesures made a new international **prototype** of meter by using platinum-iridium alloy in 1889, and **stipulated** that the distance between the marked **scales** on the prototype, measured at the zero **degree centigrade temperature**, is one meter. Copies of the new international meter prototypes were distributed to all countries for **preservation**.

　　在1875年，許多國家一同簽訂「公制公約」，共同發展公制系統與協調國際間不同單位制的轉換。而且為了使公約能實際運行，同年便在巴黎近郊設立「國際度量衡局」（Bureau international des poids et mesures，縮寫BIPM），從此全球化的公制便開始展開。「國際度量衡局」於1889年以鉑銥合金又製造了一個新的國際公尺原器，並規定在攝氏零度時，所測量到公尺原器上兩道刻度之間的距離為1米（慣稱公尺），並將新的國際公尺原器之複製品分發給各國保存。

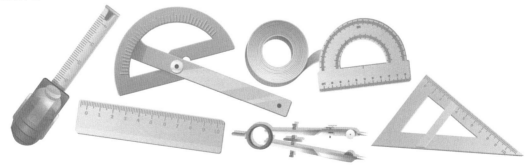

Vocabulary

sign (v.) 簽訂	global (a.) 全球化的
convention (n.) 公約	unfold (v.) 展開
jointly (ad.) 共同地	prototype (n.) 原型
coordinate (v.) 協調	stipulate (v.) 規定
conversion (n.) 轉換	scale (n.) 刻度
in order to 為了……	degree (n.) 度
operational (a.) 運行的；運轉的	centigrade (n.) 攝氏度
bureau (n.) 局	temperature (n.) 溫度
suburb (n.) 郊外	preservation (n.) 保存

Sentences

◇ The two countries **signed** a peace treaty to end the war.
兩國簽訂了和平條約來結束戰爭。

◇ Many international **conventions** were signed in Switzerland.
很多國際公約是在瑞士簽訂的。

◇ The two professors decided to **jointly** do research. 兩位教授決定共同做研究。

◇ He carefully **coordinated** a large number of organizations to work together.
他協調了很多單位來共同工作。

◇ The work of **conversion** of wind to electricity is by no means easy.
將風力轉換成電力是不容易的。

◇ **In order to** be strong, he swims every day. 為求強壯，他每天游泳。

◇ This machine is not **operational** yet. 這架機器尚未能實際運作。

◇ This **bureau** is to promote scientific research. 這個局是為了推行科學研究的。

◇ It is good to live in the **suburb**. 住在郊外是件好事。

◇ Climate change is a **global** problem. 氣候變遷是全球化的問題。

◇ An effort to find the cause of the disease was **unfolded** last week.
找出病因的努力已在上週展開。

◇ A **prototype** of the new airplane was made last month.
新飛機的原型已於上個月完成了。

◇ The government **stipulated** that everyone should wear a mask.
政府規定人人都要戴口罩。

◇ Pay attention to the **scales** of the ruler. 注意尺上的刻度。

◇ Trigonometry always talks about **degrees** of angles. 三角學是在討論角的度數。

◇ We all use **centigrade** to measure temperature these days.
我們現在都用攝氏測量溫度。

◇ The **temperature** is always high in this region. 這裡的溫度總是很高。

◇ The **preservation** of ancient civilization is important. 保存古文明是很重要的。

Translate the following sentences into Chinese

1 Many scholars signed a document asking the government to help universities.

➙

2 Many international conventions were held in Switzerland.

➙

3 This scientific discovery is a result of a joint research project.

➙

4 A project involving a large number of people needs good coordination.

➙

5 This circuit converts analog signal to digital signal.

➙

6 In order to catch the train, he gets up early in the morning.

➙

7 This machine is finally operational.

➙

8 This bureau is to take care of poor people.

↪
....

9 It is expensive to live in the suburb.

↪
....

10 Poverty is a global problem.

↪
....

11 It is not easy to produce the prototype of the new airplane.

↪
....

12 The government stipulated that children should go to school.

↪
....

13 The scales of a ruler have to be calibrated carefully.

↪
....

14 Only a small number of countries do not use centigrade to measure temperature these days.

↪
....

15 When two lines are perpendicular to each other, they form an angle of 90 degrees.

↪
....

16 Trigonometry always talks about degrees of angles.

↪
....

17 We have to pay close attention to the temperature during this process.

↪
....

18 It is important to preserve ancient civilization.

↪
....

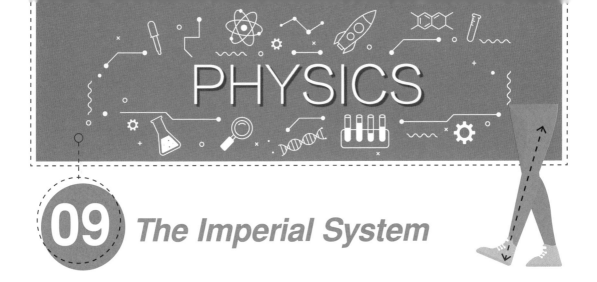

09 *The Imperial System*

Since the metric system is easy to use, it is widely **adopted** by **various** countries, but there are still a few countries in the world which use the "Imperial System." The **basic unit** of imperial length is "feet." However, how was feet determined? In a church in a certain place on a certain day of a certain year, after the **Sunday service**, the **average** length of the left foot of the first 13 **adults** who walked out was one foot (about 30.48 cm). As for "**yard**," which was commonly used by the British in the past, it was determined by a British king who straightened his hand **horizontally**, and then measured the distance between his nose and his fingers. This distance was one yard (91.44 cm). We have to say that the British really have a **sense of humor**!

由於公制單位使用方便，廣為各國採行，但世界上仍有一些國家使用「英制」。英制長度的基本單位是「英呎」。然而，英呎是怎麼訂定的呢？在某年某月某日某地的一個教堂中，主日禮拜結束以後，最先走出的十三位成人的左腳長度的平均數，就是一英呎（約30.48公分）。至於英國人過去常用的碼（yard）呢？那是一位英國國王將他的手水平伸直，然後量他鼻尖到手指之間的距離，就是一碼（91.44公分）。我們不得不說，英國人可真有幽默感！

Vocabulary

- adopt (v.) 採行；採取
- various (a.) 各個；不同的
- imperial (a.) 帝國的
- basic (a.) 基本的

- unit (n.) 單位
- Sunday service 主日禮拜
- average (a.) 平均的

- adult (n.) 成人
- yard (n.) 碼
- horizontally (ad.) 水平地
- sense of humor 幽默感

Sentences

◇ He finally **adopted** swimming as his hobby. 他最終選了游泳作為他的嗜好。

◇ He got sick because of **various** reasons. 他因為各種原因而生病。

◇ There are not many **imperial** countries in the world now. 現今世上的帝國不多了。

◇ We should pay attention to **basic** industrial technologies.
我們該注意工業的基本技術。

◇ The basic **unit** of weight is gram. 重量的基本單位是公克。

◇ A lot of people come to the **Sunday service** of this church.
很多人來參加這座教堂的主日禮拜。

◇ The **average** age of employees in this company is quite young.
這家公司職員的平均年齡很低。

◇ Only **adults** can vote. 只有成人才能選舉。

◇ **Yard** is only used in a small number of countries. 僅有少數國家使用碼。

◇ The **horizontal** axis in geometry is called the x-axis. 幾何的水平線通常被稱為 x 軸。

◇ You will be very popular if you have a good **sense of humor**.
你如有好的幽默感，就會很受人歡迎。

Translate the following sentences into Chinese

1 Music is often adopted by people as a hobby. ✎

2 He got depressed for various reasons. ✎

3 Basic science is extremely important. ✎

4 The basic unit of capacitance is Farad. ✎

5 The average income of the people of a country is not that meaningful.
✎

6 This medicine is for adults only. ✎

7 It is safer to walk horizontally. ✎

8 It is not easy to be humorous. ✎

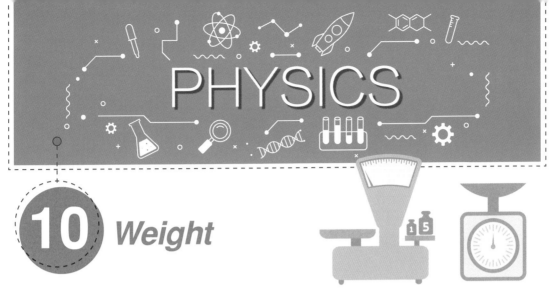

10 *Weight*

Before discussing **mass**, let's talk about **weight** first, because everyone has a better sense of weight. **Suppose** we have a bag of rice today, and its weight is 1 kg. If we measure the weight of the rice with a **spring balance**, the weight of this bag of rice is 1 kg. But if we take this bag of rice to a high mountain today and take out a **spring scale** to measure it, we will find that the weight of the rice has **decreased** a little (decreasing 1 percent with every 3.2 km **increase** in **height**). But if we measure this bag of rice with a **balance scale**, we will find that the weight of this bag of rice is the same as the weight of a 1 kg **standard weight**. If we take this bag of rice to the moon and measure it with a spring scale, the weight of the rice will only be 1/6 kg, and if we use a balance scale to measure it, the weight of this bag of rice is still the same as that of a 1 kg standard weight.

在談質量以前,我們先談重量,因為大家對重量比較有感覺。假設今天我們有一袋米,重量是1公斤重。我們試以彈簧秤測量米的重量,得到這袋米的重量是1公斤重。但是如果今天我們把這袋米拿到高山上去,又拿出彈簧秤來測量,會發現米的重量減少了一點點(隨高度每增加3.2 km而減少1%)。但是如果我們以天平秤來測量這袋米,我們會發現,這袋米和1公斤的砝碼一樣重。如果我們將這袋米帶到月球上,用彈簧秤來測量,米的重量會只有1/6公斤,而如果用天平秤來測量,這袋米仍然和1公斤的砝碼是一樣重的。

Vocabulary

mass (n.) 質量
weight (n.) 重量
suppose (v.) 假設

spring scale 彈簧秤
(= spring balance)
decrease (v.) 減少
increase (v.) 增加

height (n.) 高度
balance (n.) 平衡
balance scale 天平秤
standard weight 砝碼

Sentences

◇ In physics, **mass** is more important than **weight**. 在物理學，質量比重量更重要。

◇ **Suppose** you want to be a scientist, you must be good in mathematics.
假設你想做一個科學家，你一定要學好數學。

◇ The **spring scale** is related to the gravitational force of the earth.
彈簧秤是與地心引力有關的。

◇ As we grow older, our ability to remember things **decreases**.
年歲增加了，記憶力就減少了。

◇ As we grow older, our ability to understand things **increases**.
年歲增加了，理解力就增加了。

◇ The temperature decreases as the **height** increases.
隨著高度增加，溫度會降低。

◇ We should always keep **balance**. 我們永遠要保持平衡。

◇ A **standard weight** is always used in a balance scale. 天平秤上總是會使用砝碼。

Translate the following sentences into Chinese

1 Kids usually cannot understand the difference between mass and weight.

2 Suppose you want to be an athlete, you must be strong.

3 As a country becomes industrialized, its number of poor people decreases.

4 As a country becomes poorer, its crime rate increases.

5 There will be less people as the height increases.

6 You should always keep a balance between your income and expenditure.

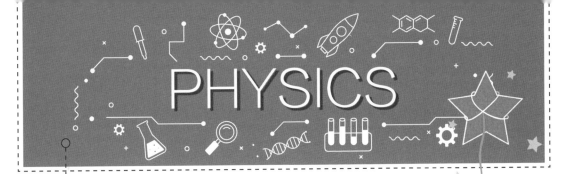

11 *Mass*

We **previously** said that the **gravity** of the moon is only 1/6 of that of the earth. So the weight of an **object** on the moon will only be 1/6 times that of the earth. Today we **assume** that there is a baseball with a mass of 360 grams and a weight of 360 grams. A baseball **pitcher** holds the ball tightly in his hand, and then uses the **force** of F to throw out the ball from a **standstill** (**speed** is 0). Finally, the pitcher throws out the ball with a speed of 150 kilometers per hour within 1 second. Suppose that the **venue** of the game is changed. The game will be played on the moon, but the same ball is used. The mass is the same as 360 grams, but the weight of the ball has become 60 grams. Suppose the pitcher still wants to throw out from his hand with a speed of 150 kilometers per hour within 1 second. Does the force he **exerts** on the ball need to be changed? The answer is: "He still only needs to **apply** F force to the ball within 1 second, neither increasing the force nor decreasing the force."

　　我們先前說道，月球的引力僅為地球的1/6倍，所以一個物體在月球上的重量也僅會是在地球上的1/6倍。今天我們假設有一顆棒球，質量是360克，重量是360克重，一個棒球投手把這個球緊緊握在手中，然後用了F的力道，將球由靜止（速度為0）向外投出，結果這顆球最後被投手在1秒內以時速150公里的速度投出。今天如果比賽的場地改變了，改換到月球上比賽了，但用的還是同樣的球，質量一樣是360克，但是球的重量卻變成60克重。假如這位投手仍想要把這顆球在1秒內從手中以時速150公里的速度投出，那他對這顆球施加的力道需要改變嗎？答案是：「他在1秒內仍然只需要對球施加F的力道，不增也不減。」

Vocabulary

previously (ad.) 先前	standstill (n.) 靜止；停止
gravity (n.) 引力	speed (n.) 速度
object (n.) 物體	venue (n.) 場地
assume (v.) 假設	exert (v.) 施加
pitcher (n.) 棒球投手	apply (v.) 運用；施加
force (n.) 力	

Sentences

◇ **Previously**, he was interested in electrical engineering. 先前，他對電機有興趣。

◇ The **gravity** of the earth is very important. 地球引力很重要。

◇ This is a heavy **object**. 這是一個重的物體。

◇ Let us **assume** that the power supply is a steady one. 假設這個電源供應很穩定。

◇ He is a good **pitcher**. 他是一個好的棒球投手。

◇ If no **force** is exerted on an object, its status will not be changed.
如果無力施加在一個物體之下，它的狀態不會改變。

◇ A **standstill** object remains standstill if no force is applied to it.
如果沒有力施加在一個靜止的物體上，它會維持靜止。

◇ When you drive a car, you must be aware of its **speed**.
如果你在開車，你一定要知道車子的速度。

◇ I do not know the **venue** of the conference. 我不知道會議的場地。

◇ You should **exert** pressure on the valve. 你應該在這活門上施力。

◇ It is hard to **apply** relativity theory to engineering.
要將相對論用在工業上是很難的。

Translate the following sentences into Chinese

1 Previously, he was a mathematician.

2 It is lucky for us that the gravity of the earth exists.

3 This is a valuable object.

4 Let us assume that the initial voltage is high.

5 If you want to move an object, you must exert force on it.

6 We have the high speed rail system now.

7 I do not know the venue of the game.

8 You should exert pressure on air.

9 It is hard to apply the Fourier transform to solve this problem.

PHYSICS

12 Gravitational Force

As we mentioned in the previous chapter, the so-called "weight" refers to the gravitational force at the place where the object is **subjected**. Therefore, objects will only **produce** weight in **environments** with **gravitational forces**, and the same object will have different weights in environments with different gravitational forces. So we can also say that the **essence** of weight is actually a **performance** of force. But what is gravity? In fact, we live in gravity every day. Everyone has heard the story that Newton was hit by an apple and discovered **universal gravity**. The apples will fall from the tree because the apple is **attracted** by the gravity of the earth. Therefore it will fall towards the ground.

我們在前節就有提過，所謂的「重量」，就是指物體受到所在之處的引力大小。因此，物體在具有引力的環境下才會產生重量，而同一個物體在不同引力的環境下也會有不同的重量。所以我們也可以說，重量的本質其實就是一種力的表現。可是什麼是引力？其實我們每天都生活在引力當中，大家都聽過牛頓被蘋果打中而發現了萬有引力的故事。蘋果會從樹上掉下來，是因為蘋果受到地球的引力吸引，所以才會朝地面落下。

Vocabulary

subject (v.) 征服；使臣服

produce (v.) 產生

environment (n.) 環境

gravitational force 引力

essence (n.) 本質

performance (n.) 表現

universal (a.) 普世的；宇宙的

universal gravity 萬有引力

attract (v.) 吸引

◇ The village was **subjected** to a very large damage due to the storm.
這個村莊因為暴風雨受到很大的損害。

◇ Taiwan **produces** a lot of chips. 台灣生產很多晶片。

◇ We should pay attention to our **environment**. 我們應該注意我們的環境。

◇ We are all influenced by the **gravitational force** of the earth.
我們都受到地球引力的影響。

◇ In **essence**, his idea is very simple. 實質上，他的想法很簡單。

◇ His **performance** is excellent. 他表現傑出。

◇ Newton discovered the Law of **Universal** Gravitation. 牛頓發現了萬有引力定律。

◇ We are **attracted** by the gravitational force of the earth. 我們被地球引力吸引。

 Translate the following sentences into Chinese

1 The difficult examination subjected him great harm.
....

2 Wind and sunlight produce electric power.
....

3 We should protect our environment when we try to promote economy.
....

4 Without the gravitational force of the earth, we will all be floating in the air.
....

5 In essence, industrial technologies are based upon science.
....

6 Wireless communication is a performance of electromagnetic waves.
....

7 The discovery of the Law of Universal Gravitation is now taught in middle
schools.
....

8 A lot of young people are attracted by the electrical engineering because they
want to understand how radio works.
....

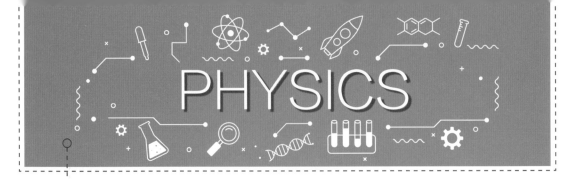

13 *Deformation*

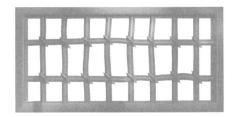

The so-called "deformation" refers to the phenomenon that the shape of the object itself changes when the object is subjected to external forces such as pulling or tearing. Any object can produce deformation, and there is no object that does not produce deformation. It is just that the difference caused by deformation may not be obvious. Some objects have more obvious deformation, such as the deformation of a spring caused by contraction and elongation. The result of deformation for some objects is not so obvious. Some cannot even be observed with the eyes. After the external force is removed, not all the deformed objects can be restored to their original shape. For example, suppose you use your feet to squash an aluminum can with great force. When your feet leave the aluminum can, the aluminum can will not return to its original shape by itself. But objects as springs, rubber bands, elastic bands, etc. will go back to their original shapes. These objects whose original shapes can be restored may be called elastic materials or elastic objects.

所謂「形變」是指當物體受到拉、扯等外力作用時，造成物體本身的形狀發生改變的現象。任何物體都能產生形變，不產生形變的物體是不存在的，只是明不明顯的差異而已。有些物體的形變比較明顯，如彈簧的縮短和拉長。而有的物體的形變就不那麼明顯了，有的甚至無法用眼睛觀察到。而產生形變後的物體在外力移除後，也不是所有物體都能恢復成原狀。像你可以用力把鋁罐踩扁，當你的腳離開鋁罐後，鋁罐並不會自行恢復原狀。但像彈簧、橡皮筋或鬆緊帶等物體就會了。這些形變後可恢復的物體，我們就稱之為彈性材料或彈性物體。

Vocabulary

- deformation (n.) 形變
- refer (v.) 指涉（＋ to）
- phenomenon (n.) 現象
- shape (n.) 形狀
- be subjected to 遭受……
- external (a.) 外面的
- pull (v.) 拉
- tear (v.) 撕；扯
- contraction (n.) 縮短
- elongation (n.) 拉長
- obvious (a.) 明顯的
- observe (v.) 觀察
- remove (v.) 移除
- restore (v.) 恢復
- original (a.) 原來的；起初的
- squash (v.) 壓扁
- aluminum (n.) 鋁
- rubber (n.) 橡皮
- band (n.) 圈
- elastic (a.) 有彈性的
- material (n.) 材料

Sentences

◇ The **deformation** of parts in a machine is a serious matter.
機器內部零組件的形變是一件嚴重的事。

◇ Astrology **refers** to the study of the universe. 天文學是指研究宇宙的學問。

◇ This is indeed a peculiar **phenomenon**. 這真是一個奇特的現象。

◇ This object has a complicated **shape**. 這個物體的形狀很複雜。

◇ This object will **be subjected to** heavy pressure when it is processed.
這個材料在製作過程中，會受到很大的壓力。

◇ We would like our machine not to be influenced by the **external** environment.
我們希望這架機器不受外界環境的影響。

◇ It is difficult to **pull** a heavy rock. 拉一塊重的石頭是很困難的。

◇ Do not **tear** down any page of this book. 不要撕下這本書的任何一頁。

◇ This tube can be **contracted** and **elongated**. 這個管子可以縮短或拉長。

◇ His answer is **obviously** wrong. 他的答案很明顯是錯誤的。

◇ In an experiment, one should always **observe** all of the results.
在實驗中，我們應該觀察所有的結果。

◇ After you remove the **pressure**, observe what will happen.
在移除壓力以後，觀察會發生什麼事。

◇ It is not easy to **restore** the environment after the fire. 在火災之後，不易使環境恢復。

◇ This is the **original** version of the book. 這是這本書的原始版本。

◇ Sometimes, we have to **squash** a sheet of metal. 有時我們需要壓扁一片金屬。

◇ **Aluminum** is a kind of metal. 鋁是一種金屬。

◇ **Rubber bands** are used in many industrial products. 很多工業產品都用了橡皮圈。

◇ We need **elastic materials** in some machines. 有的機械需要彈性的材料。

1   Deformation of parts in a machine must be avoided.

2   Biology refers to the study of living things.

3   This phenomenon is well known in the scientific community.

4   In the old days, horses were used to pull carts.

5   Do not tear down the picture on the wall.

6   This object has a unique shape.

7   This country was subjected heavy losses as a storm hit it.

8   When we design a machine, we must consider its external environment.

9   This tube can be neither contracted nor elongated.

10   A good scientist observes things which ordinary people do not notice.

11   There is nothing wrong with this computer.

12   Be careful when you remove the cover of the box.

13   The factory has restored its production after a problem was solved.

14   The original version of the book was lost.

15   The shape of this object will not change.

16   Aluminum is a useful metal.

17   Every household uses rubber bands.

18   The process of producing elastic materials is often quite complicated.

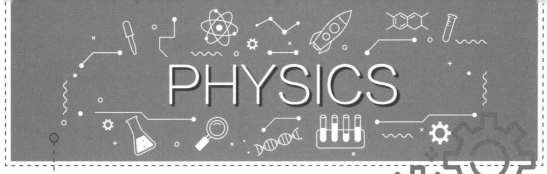

14 Mechanics

Mechanics was a **branch** in physics and was **developed** very early. In **nature**, the moving or being standstill of all objects is within the **realm** of mechanics. The movement of large objects, such as **celestial objects** and the movement of small objects, such as electrons, which are **invisible** to us, all need to be **analyzed** by mechanics. Of course, at the very beginning, physicists studied movement of objects from the view of force. But, every movement will **exhaust energy**. For us human beings, even **breathing** and sleeping which are light actions will **continuously** exhaust energy. In other words, there is a close **relationship** between movement and energy. Therefore, physicists started to **investigate** the movement of objects from the **viewpoint** of energy.

力學是物理學的一個分支,很早就被發展出來。自然界中所有物質的運動或不動均脫離不了力學的範疇,從大至天體運動,到小至肉眼無法看到的電子運動,均需要使用力學來分析。當然,一開始物理學家是從「力」的觀點來研究物質的運動現象,但任何物體只要「運動」就必然會消耗能量。以人類來說,即使像呼吸、睡覺這種輕而易舉的事情,都會不停消耗掉能量。也就是說物質的運動與能量是密不可分的,因此到後來,物理學家也開始從「能量」的觀點來探討物體的運動現象。

Vocabulary

mechanics (n.) 力學
branch (n.) 分支
develop (v.) 發展
nature (n.) 大自然
realm (n.) 範疇
celestial objects 天體

invisible (a.) 不可見的;看不到的
analyze (v.) 分析
exhaust (v.) 消耗
energy (n.) 能量

breathe (v.) 呼吸
continuously (ad.) 不斷地
relationship (n.) 關係
investigate (v.) 探討
viewpoint 觀點

 Sentences

◇ **Mechanics** involves a lot of mathematics. 力學牽涉到很多數學。

◇ Algebra is a **branch** of mathematics. 代數是數學的一個分支。

◇ We should work hard to **develop** science and technology. 我們應該努力發展科技。

◇ It is hard to understand **nature**. 瞭解大自然是很困難的。

◇ The study of DNA is in the **realm** of life science. DNA 隸屬生命科學的範疇。

◇ It is always amazing to see the movement of **celestial objects**.
看天體運行總是令人驚奇。

◇ Electrons actually are **invisible** to us. 電子是看不見的。

◇ We should carefully **analyze** the data before we make any conclusion.
在下結論以前，我們應先仔細地分析資料。

◇ We should not **exhaust** too much energy. 我們不應過度消耗能量。

◇ It is hard to store **energy**. 儲存能量是很難的。

◇ **Breathing** is a sign of life. 呼吸是有生命的象徵。

◇ The earth **continuously** rotates. 地球不斷地旋轉。

◇ There is a close **relationship** between communication and mathematics.
通訊和數學有密切的關係。

◇ We should **investigate** why this machine is so good.
我們該探討為何這架機器如此之好。

◇ He investigates the problem from the **viewpoint** of optics.
他從光學的觀點來探討這個問題。

 Translate the following sentences into Chinese

1   Mechanics is quite fundamental in physics.

   ✍

2   Geometry is a branch of mathematics.

   ✍

3 We should work hard to develop our industries.

☞

4 It is almost impossible to control nature.

☞

5 The study of algorithms is in the realm of computer science.

☞

6 It is always amazing to know how a precision machine is made.

☞

7 Protons actually are invisible to us.

☞

8 We should carefully analyze why the machine fails to work properly.

☞

9 We should not exhaust too much energy.

☞

10 The rich people exhaust much more energy than the poor people.

☞

11 Breathing is of vital importance to us.

☞

12 The sun continuously rises in the east.

☞

13 There is a relationship between music and mathematics.

☞

14 We should investigate the origin of the plague.

☞

15 He investigates the problem from the viewpoint of social science.

☞

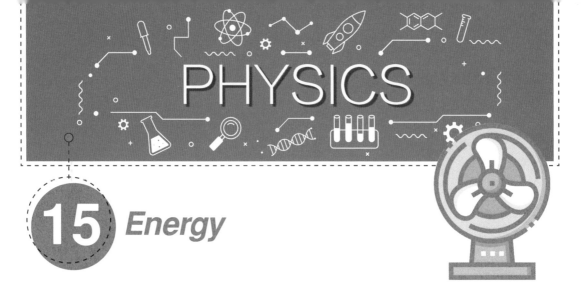

PHYSICS

15 *Energy*

Before discussing the relationship between energy and movement, we must first understand what energy is. The word "energy" came from the Greek word "ἐνέργεια" which was originally suggested by Aristotle. At that time, it meant the **potential capability** to do work or take action. It was later **introduced** into physics and became the energy which we all now understand. The **thermal** energy, light energy, electric energy, **nuclear** energy and chemical energy can all be called energy. Their **functions** are just expressed in **various** forms. Yet, whatever the energy is, it must possess the ability to make an object complete a certain work. For example, the electric energy can cause an electric fan to **rotate**. The thermal energy can make food well cooked. Therefore, in physics, any physical **quantity** which can do work is energy.

在學習能量與物質運動的關係之前,我們首先要知道什麼是能量(energy)。「能量」一詞源自於希臘語ἐνέργεια,率先由亞里斯多德提出,在當時就是指能使工作或活動發生的潛在能力。後來才被引進物理學用以表示我們所知的能量。熱能、光能、電能、核能、化學能等都可以通稱為能量。他們的功能只是以不同的形式呈現出來而已。然而,不管是哪一種能量,都具有使物體完成某件工作(work)的能力。像電能可使電風扇轉動,熱能可以煮熟食物。因此在物理學上,凡是可以作功(work)的物理量就是能量。

Vocabulary

potential
(a.) 潛在的 / (n.) 潛力
capability (n.) 能力
introduce (v.) 引進

thermal (a.) 熱的;熱量的
nuclear (n.) 原子核的
function (n.) 功能

various (a.) 不同的
rotate (v.) 旋轉
quantity (n.) 量

Sentences

◇ He has the **potential** to become a great mathematician. 他有成為偉大數學家的潛力。

◇ He has the **capability** to solve this problem. 他有解決這問題的能力。

◇ He **introduced** algorithms into computer science. 他將演算法引入電腦科學。

◇ Engineers are working hard to use the **thermal** energy. 工程師在努力設法利用熱能。

◇ People are always afraid to use **nuclear** energy. 人們總是害怕使用核能。

◇ The **function** of this machine is unknown. 無人知道這架機器的功能。

◇ There are **various** theories to explain this strange experimental result.
有不同的理論來解釋這個奇怪的實驗結果。

◇ **Rotation** often causes wind. 旋轉常會造成風。

◇ **Quantity** and quality are both important. 量和質同樣重要。

Translate the following sentences into Chinese

1 This country has the potential to become an industrialized country.

    ↪

2 He has the capability to design complicated software.

    ↪

3 He introduced his students into astrology.

    ↪

4 It is relatively easy to use the thermal energy.

    ↪

5 People should be very careful when they use nuclear energy.

    ↪

6 Different machines have different functions.

    ↪

7 Various machines have been designed to perform the same task.

    ↪

8 If a part of the machine rotates, the designer has to be very careful because
    rotation causes many troubles. ↪

9 There are many physical quantities in physics, which a student has to learn.

    ↪

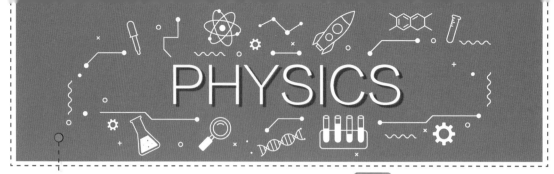

PHYSICS

16 Kinetic Energy

Let us look at another example. Suppose that there are a bicycle and a truck carrying siltstone and they are both moving forward with the same speed. Let us assume that the speed is 30 km per hour. If we were hit by those vehicles, which result will be more serious? Although the two vehicles are of the same speed, the mass of the truck carrying siltstones is much larger. The results of being hit by these two vehicles are entirely different. Being hit by the bicycle head-on, we may get abrasion or bruise. A more serious injury may be a broken bone. But, you may lose your life if you are hit by that truck. This example tells us, under the condition with the same speed, the object with larger mass has larger kinetic energy.

我們再舉另外一個例子來看，假設在馬路上有一輛腳踏車與一輛砂石車，都是以相同的速度向前行駛。我們認定他們都是以時速30公里的速度前進好了。假設我們被這不同的兩輛車撞到，哪一個後果會比較嚴重呢？雖然兩輛車都是以相同的速度前進，但是砂石車的質量比腳踏車的質量大很多，所以被這兩輛車撞到的結果也會大不相同。被腳踏車正面撞上，有可能是擦傷、瘀青，嚴重一些可能會骨折。若是被砂石車撞上，可能就一命嗚呼了。這個例子告訴我們，雖然是速度相同的情況，具有愈大質量的物體，所具有的動能也就愈大。

Vocabulary

siltstone (n.) 砂石	abrasion (n.) 擦傷
speed (n.) 速度	bruise (n.) 瘀青
assume (v.) 假設	condition (n.) 情況，條件
serious (a.) 嚴重的	kinetic energy 動能

Sentences

◇ The **siltstones** are often used in construction work. 建造工程中常用到砂石。

◇ You cannot drive over **speed**. 你不能超速駕駛。

◇ Let us **assume** that the temperature is very high. 假設溫度很高。

◇ He was **seriously** injured in the car accident. 他在車禍中受重傷。

◇ There were only **abrasion** and **bruise** on his legs. 他腿部僅有擦傷和瘀青。

◇ His **condition** is improving. 他的情況在進步之中。

◇ We use **kinetic energy** to produce electricity. 我們利用動能發電。

Translate the following sentences into Chinese

1 The speed of electromagnetic waves is the same as the speed of light.

　↭

2 Let us assume that the condition is under control.

　↭

3 His condition is now very serious.

　↭

4 Abrasion and bruise are not serious.

　↭

5 This machine works under the condition that the temperature is very low.

　↭

6 Kinetic energy is important for our daily life.

　↭

PHYSICS

17 The Transfer of Kinetic Energy

The so-called kinetic energy is the energy obtained when an object is moving, or the result of transferring the work done by a moving object to another object. In other words, every moving object **possesses** kinetic energy. Besides, through doing work, the kinetic energy of a moving object can be **transferred** to another object. **Imagine** that we are playing **billiard**. When we use the **pool cue** to hit a ball, the ball will move due to the force **applied** on it. The work done by the force will be transformed into energy and this energy is the kinetic energy received by the ball. We may also force a **dodgeball** to **roll** towards a basketball. After the dodgeball hits the basketball, the basketball will roll because it was hit. Now, we can say that the rolling dodge ball possesses kinetic energy and after hitting the basketball, the dodgeball transfers its kinetic energy to the basketball.

所謂的動能（kinetic energy），是指物質在運動時所得到的能量，或者是一個物體在運動中對另外一個物體產生作功的效果。換句話說，任何運動中的物體必具有動能，而且透過作用可以使一個物體的動能再轉移到另一個物體上。想像我們在玩撞球，當用球桿撞球時，球因受力而運動，那力對球作功轉換出來的能量就是球所獲得的動能了。或者，我們拿一顆躲避球朝著另一顆靜止的籃球滾過去，當躲避球撞上籃球之後，籃球也會因為受到撞擊而向前滾動。此時我們可以說，正在滾動的躲避球具有動能，在碰撞籃球之後，躲避球將它本身所具有的動能轉移給籃球了。

Vocabulary

possess (v.) 具有；擁有
transfer (v.) 移轉
imagine (v.) 想像

billiard (n.) 撞球
pool cue 球桿
apply (v.) 起作用；應用

dodge (v.) 躲避／
dodgeball (n.) 躲避球
roll (v.) 滾動

Sentences

◇ A standing still object does not **possess** kinetic energy. 靜止不動的物體不具有動能。

◇ Energy can be **transferred** to another object. 能量可以被移轉到別的物體。

◇ It is hard to **imagine** that this machine is so good. 很難想像這架機器如此精良。

◇ Rich people often have a **billiard** pool table in their homes.
富人常在家中設有撞球台。

◇ Once you know how to **apply** mathematics, many engineering problems can be easily solved. 一旦你知道如何應用數學，很多工程問題就會迎刃而解。

◇ Do not **dodge** my question. 不要躲避我的問題。

◇ This is a **rolling** machine. 這是一個捲板機。

Translate the following sentences into Chinese

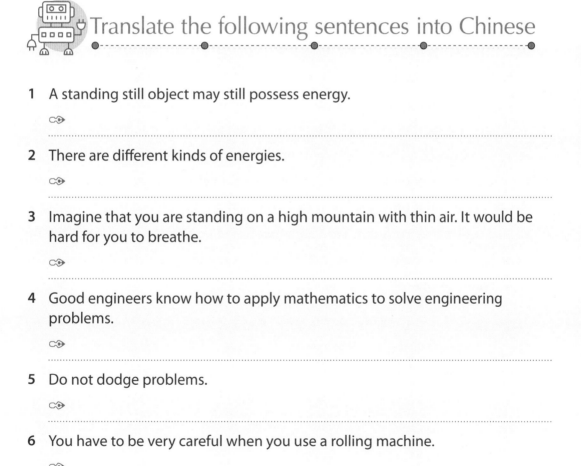

1 A standing still object may still possess energy.

　⤷ ....

2 There are different kinds of energies.

　⤷ ....

3 Imagine that you are standing on a high mountain with thin air. It would be hard for you to breathe.

　⤷ ....

4 Good engineers know how to apply mathematics to solve engineering problems.

　⤷ ....

5 Do not dodge problems.

　⤷ ....

6 You have to be very careful when you use a rolling machine.

　⤷ ....

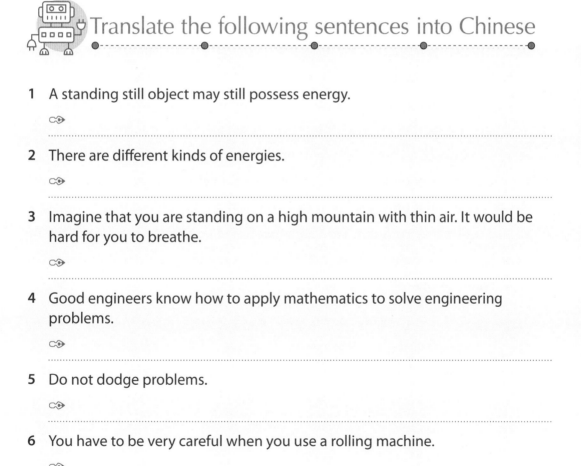

PHYSICS | 17

The Transfer of Kinetic Energy

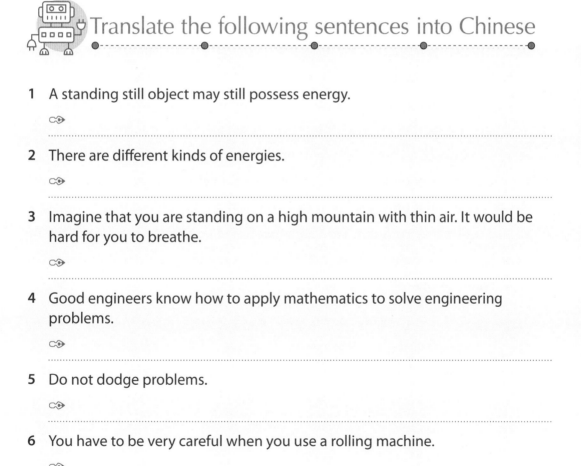

151

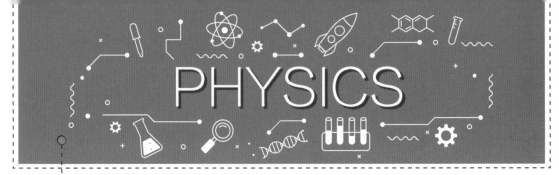

18 *Potential Energy*

After we understand what kinetic energy is, we will now introduce **potential energy**. The so-called potential energy is the energy **obtained** by an object located in a **particular** location. In

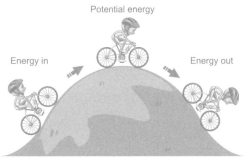

Potential energy

Energy in

Energy out

simpler terms, we may say that potential energy is an energy **related** to location. If the energy is only related to the location in the **space**, it can be **defined** as the potential energy. In other words, so far as potential energy is concerned, it is not essential to ask how the object reaches the location. It is neither important to know how much time it takes to reach that location. We only consider how much energy the object possesses when it is at that location. Therefore it is important to **select** a **reference point**. Usually, the reference point is the **horizon**. We may also use the position before the object is moved as the reference point. We will know how large the potential energy by comparing the locations before and after the moving. The potential energy is actually a **relative quantity**.

　　當我們對動能有一定的了解後，接下來就來介紹什麼是位能吧！所謂的位能（potential energy），是指物體在特定位置上所儲存的能量。簡單來說，就是與位置有關的能量，任何形式的能量若僅與空間中的位置有關，就可定義成位能。也就是說，對位能而言，物體是怎麼到達這個位置並不重要，花了多久時間也不重要，因為我們只考慮這個物體在目前的這個位置上，到底具有多少的能量。因此選擇物體所在位置的參照點就很重要了。通常這個參照點會是地平面，也可以是物體運動前的位置。將參照點與後來物體所在的位置比較後，就可以知道物體的位能大小，故物體的位能大小是一種相對量值。

Vocabulary

potential energy 位能	select (v.) 選擇
obtain (v.) 得到	reference point 參照點
particular (a.) 特定的	horizon (n.) 水平線；地平線
related (a.) 有關的	relative (a.) 相對的
space (n.) 空間	quantity (n.) 量
define (v.) 定義	

Sentences

◇ It is rather difficult to know the precise meaning of **potential energy**.
要知道位能的精確意義是很困難的。

◇ Can you **obtain** the main idea of designing this analog circuit?
你能得到設計這個類比線路的主要概念嗎？

◇ You must know the **particular** temperature of this process.
你一定要知道這個製程的特定溫度。

◇ Computer science is **related** to mathematics. 電腦科學和數學有關。

◇ His working **space** is very small. 他的工作空間很小。

◇ This term is not **defined**. 這個名詞沒有定義。

◇ We must **select** a good adviser. 我們一定要選擇一個好的指導教授。

◇ The **reference point** is critical for computation. 在計算時，參照點是很重要的。

◇ Everyone knows what the **horizon** is. 人人都知道水平線是什麼。

◇ As compared with other students, he is **relatively** smart.
和別的學生相比，他是相對聰明的。

◇ The **quantity** of rice produced in this country is very large.
這個國家米的產量很大。

1 Potential energy is quite useful for every country.

2 You can obtain potential energy by moving an object to a high place.

3 You must know the particular person who designed this machine.

4 His boss keeps his working space warm.

5 Material science is related to both chemical and mechanical engineering.

6 You must clearly define the product of your company.

7 We must select a good place to construct your house.

8 When you make some statements, you must give the reference point precisely.

9 The ocean is below the horizon.

10 Only a small number of people understand the relativity theory proposed by Einstein.

11 The quantity of the output of this company is small. But the quality of its output is exceedingly good.

19 Wave

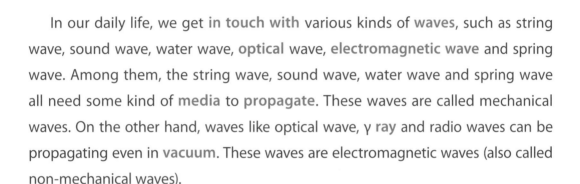

In our daily life, we get **in touch with** various kinds of **waves**, such as string wave, sound wave, water wave, **optical** wave, **electromagnetic wave** and spring wave. Among them, the string wave, sound wave, water wave and spring wave all need some kind of **media** to **propagate**. These waves are called mechanical waves. On the other hand, waves like optical wave, γ **ray** and radio waves can be propagating even in **vacuum**. These waves are electromagnetic waves (also called non-mechanical waves).

在我們日常生活中能接觸到各式各樣的波，如繩波、聲波、水波、光波、電磁波和彈簧波。其中：如繩波、聲波、水波、彈簧波等需要介質來傳遞波，像這樣的波就稱為力學波。反之，其他如光波、γ射線、無線電波等不需介質，意即在真空中也能傳播的波，像這樣的波是電磁波（又稱為非力學波或非機械波）。

Vocabulary

in touch with 接觸	media (n.) 介質；媒介
wave (n.) 波	propagate (v.) 傳播
optical (a.) 光學的	ray (n.) 射線
electromagnetic wave 電磁波	vacuum (n.) 真空

Sentences

◇ He got **in touch with** many mathematicians when he was in college.
他在大學時接觸了很多數學家。

◇ The science of **waves** involves mathematics. 光波的學問牽涉到數學。

◇ Many sophisticated machines use **optics**. 很多高級機器用了光學。

◇ It is really hard to truly understand **electromagnetic waves**. 電磁波是很難懂的。

◇ It is amazing to know that electromagnetic waves can propagate without any **media**. 電磁波無需介質也能傳播，真是神奇。

◇ Many waves are **propagating** in the air without being noticed by us.
空氣中有很多波在傳播，但我們不知道。

◇ We are familiar with **X-ray**. 我們都對 X 光很熟悉。

◇ Many machines nowadays use **vacuum** technology. 現今很多新的機器用了真空技術。

Translate the following sentences into Chinese

1 I have never been in touch with scientists.

ເ∽

2 We all have seen waves. Yet we barely understand them.

ເ∽

3 Optics is now used in measurement.

ເ∽

4 The speed of electromagnetic waves is the fastest.

ເ∽

5 Electromagnetic wave is the only wave which can propagate without any media. ເ∽

6 When waves propagate in the air, they are often reflected.

ເ∽

7 X-ray machines are used in all hospitals now.

ເ∽

8 I learned how to use vacuum tubes when I was in college years ago.

ເ∽

PHYSICS

20 *Hertz*

Hertz, through a **series** of **experiments**, not only **proved** the **existence** of electromagnetic waves, but also determined their **wave lengths** and **frequencies**. He also proved that the speed of electromagnetic waves is the same as the speed of light, and these waves can **penetrate** air, **reflect** and **refract**. Besides, as he was doing research on electromagnetic waves, he also developed methods to **transmit** and **receive** electromagnetic waves. His research **stimulated** the **application** of electromagnetic waves to **communication**, **global positioning system** and **internet**. It is impossible for us to **avoid** using **radio broadcasting**, **television** and **cell phones** at present which are all examples of applications of wireless electromagnetic waves in our daily lives. It was a **pity** that Hertz died early. He died when he was only thirty-six years old. Many people believe that if he lived longer, he must have been the first Nobel Prize winner in physics.

　　赫茲透過一系列的實驗，不但證明電磁波的存在，測定出電磁波的波長、頻率，最後更證實電磁波與光有相同的速度，能夠穿透空氣，同時也有反射、折射等現象。此外，他在研究電磁波時，同時發展出電磁波發射、接收的方法，激發了後來電磁波在通訊、導航、網路的發展。在當今的生活中，我們絕對離不開廣播、電視、手機等，而這些也只是無線電波應用在日常生活中的諸多實例之一而已。可惜的是，赫茲英年早逝，他去世的時候才36歲而已。事實上，很多人都認為如果他多活幾年的話，第一屆的諾貝爾物理學獎，一定非他莫屬！

 Vocabulary

series (n.) 系列	application (n.) 應用
experiment (n.) 實驗	communication (n.) 通訊
prove (v.) 證明	global (a.) 全球性的
existence (n.) 存在	positioning (n.) 定位
wave length 波長	system (n.) 系統
frequency (n.) 頻率	internet (n.) 網際網路
penetrate (v.) 穿透	avoid (v.) 避免
reflect (v.) 反射	radio (n.) 收音機
refract (v.) 折射	broadcasting (n.) 廣播
transmit (v.) 發射	television (n.) 電視
receive (v.) 接受	cell phone (n.) 手機
stimulate (v.) 激發	pity (n.) 可惜；憾事

 Sentences

◇ After a **series** of failures, he finally succeeded. 經過一連串的失敗之後，他終於成功了。

◇ **Experiments** proved that his theory is correct. 實驗證明了他的理論是正確的。

◇ He cannot **prove** this theorem. 他無法證明這個定理。

◇ It is important to prove the **existence** of a solution of this problem.
證明這個問題有解是很重要的。

◇ The **wave length** of a signal is reverse to its frequency. 訊號的波長和頻率成反比。

◇ The **frequency** of human voice is actually quite low. 人聲的頻率其實是很低的。

◇ Electromagnetic waves cannot **penetrate** metal. 電磁波無法穿透金屬。

◇ If a wave reaches an object which cannot go through, it will **reflect** back.
如果波遇到一個它不能穿透的物體，它會反射回來。

◇ The **refraction** of a signal often happens. 訊號的折射常常發生的。

◇ The **transmission** of a signal is always the first step of communication.
發射訊號是通訊的第一步。

◇ Receiver **receives** the signal and also amplifies it. 接收器接收訊號，也將它放大。

◇ Curiosity **stimulates** the desire to find the answer. 好奇心激發尋找答案的慾望。

◇ The **application** of trigonometry to communication is really amazing.
將三角應用到通訊上是很神奇的。

◇ It is not easy to understand wireless **communication**. 要懂得無線通訊是很難的。

◇ This is a **global** problem. 這是一個全球性的問題。

◇ We need a precise **positioning system**. 我們需要一個精確的定位系統。

◇ We should **avoid** making wrong conclusions. 我們要避免做錯誤的結論。

◇ We are all familiar with **radio broadcasting**, yet only a few people know the science behind radio. 我們都熟悉收音機廣播，但很少人知道收音機的原理。

◇ A **television** is actually a very complicated machine.
電視機事實上是一種相當複雜的機械。

◇ The equipment for **cell phones** are all expensive. 手機所用到的設備都很昂貴。

◇ It is a **pity** that many brilliant scientists died so young.
可惜很多傑出科學家都英年早逝。

Translate the following sentences into Chinese

1 He is now giving a series of lectures.

   ☞

2 Students should learn how to perform experiments.

   ☞

3 Only mathematicians can prove theorems.

   ☞

4 In mathematics, we often hear the term "there exists." Not many people can understand the meaning of it.

   ☞

5 The wave length of light is always an important research topic.

   ☞

6 The frequency of cell phone signals is quite high.

   ☞

7   Sound can penetrate walls. ᴄ⊕

8   We all have the experience of the reflection of sound.
    ᴄ⊕

9   Light refracts. ᴄ⊕

10 There is a transmitter in our mobile phone.
    ᴄ⊕

11 A receiver uses an antenna to receive the signal.
    ᴄ⊕

12 The desire to have excellent achievements stimulates hard work.
    ᴄ⊕

13 It is difficult to apply physics to solve engineering problems if you are not
    good at physics. ᴄ⊕

14 Communication involves mathematics and physics.
    ᴄ⊕

15 Climate change is a global problem.
    ᴄ⊕

16 The global positioning system which we are using now is good enough for us.
    ᴄ⊕

17 We should avoid following others blindly.
    ᴄ⊕

18 It is easy to interfere with radio broadcasting.
    ᴄ⊕

19 Television was invented before WWII.
    ᴄ⊕

20 Cell phones are used everywhere now.
    ᴄ⊕

21 It is a pity that not many people truly understand science.
    ᴄ⊕

research 研究 C13

resolution 決議 P6

respond 反應 B15

restore 恢復 P13

result 結果 B4

revolution 革命 C19, P6

revolve 旋轉 C9

right 權利 C6

role 角色 B6

roll 滾動 P17

root 根部 B5

rotate 旋轉 P15

roughly 大約 B13

royal 皇家的 B7

rubber 橡皮 P13

Russian 俄羅斯的；俄羅斯人 B3

rust 生鏽 C20

S

saliva 唾液 B18

salt 鹽 C1, C2

satisfy 滿意 C2

scale 刻度 P8

science 科學 C5

sea-level 海平面 C19

season 季節 P2

sect 教派 C6

seed 種子 B1

select 選擇 P18

sense 意識；意義 B20

sense of humor 幽默感 P9

series 連串；系列 C16, P20

serious 嚴重的 B12, P2, P16

shake 晃動 P4

shape 形狀 C12, P13

side effect 後遺症 B10

sign 簽訂 P8

signal 信號；訊號 B15

significant 重要的 B5, C9

siltstone 砂石 P16

situation 情況 B20

slavery 奴隸制度 C6

small intestine 小腸 B18

smallpox 天花 B7

smell 氣味 C17

society 學會；社會 B7

sodium 鈉 C2

so far as . . . is concerned 對……而言 C12

soil 泥土 B6

social justice 社會正義 C6

solid 固體 C12

solve 解決 B12

sophisticated 精密的；複雜的 P3

space 空間 C3, P18

speed 速度 C9, P11, P16

spring scale 彈簧秤 P10

specimen 標本 B2

sperm cell 精子細胞 B3

spine 脊椎 B16

spread 散布；傳開 B8

squash 壓扁 P13

stable 穩定的 C17

standard 標準 C11, P6

standard weight 砝碼 P10

standstill 靜止的 P11

state 狀態 B20

statement 說明 C5

steel 鋼鐵 C12

stimulation 刺激 B15

stipulate 規定 P8

stomach 胃 B18

stone 石頭 B1

strep throat 咽喉炎 B9

strike 撞擊 C10

subject 受到 P12, P13

suburb 郊外 P8

suppose 假設 P10

surgeon 外科醫生 C14

surround 繞著 C9

substance 物質 B4, C1

suggest 提出 C16

suitable 適合的 C1

Sunday service 主日禮拜 P9

survive 生存 C3

synthesis 合成 C18

sweat 出汗 B19

swing 擺動 P4

syndrome 症侯群 C6

syphilis 梅毒 B10

Linking English

教你讀懂理工英語：完整剖析生物、化學、物理英語

2021年8月初版　　　　　　　　　　　　　　　　　定價：新臺幣320元
有著作權・翻印必究
Printed in Taiwan.

著　　者	李　家　同	
	周　照　庭	
叢書編輯	賴　祖　兒	
內文排版	劉　秋　筑	
封面設計	Lady GuGu	

出　版　者	聯經出版事業股份有限公司
地　　　址	新北市汐止區大同路一段369號1樓
叢書編輯電話	(02)86925588轉5317
台北聯經書房	台北市新生南路三段94號
電　　　話	(02)23620308
台中分公司	台中市北區崇德路一段198號
暨門市電話	(04)22312023
台中電子信箱	e-mail：linking2@ms42.hinet.net
郵政劃撥帳戶第0100559-3號	
郵撥電話	(02)23620308
印　刷　者	文聯彩色製版印刷有限公司
總　經　銷	聯合發行股份有限公司
發　行　所	新北市新店區寶橋路235巷6弄6號2樓
電　　　話	(02)29178022

副總編輯	陳　逸　華
總編輯	涂　豐　恩
總經理	陳　芝　宇
社　長	羅　國　俊
發行人	林　載　爵

行政院新聞局出版事業登記證局版臺業字第0130號

國家圖書館出版品預行編目資料

教你讀懂理工英語：完整剖析生物、化學、物理英語/
李家同、周照庭著 . 初版 . 新北市 . 聯經 . 2021年8月 . 168面 .
19×26公分（Linking English）
ISBN 978-957-08-5875-4（平裝）

1.英語 2.讀本

805.18　　　　　　　　　　　　　　　　　　110008635